Brewster's Millions

The Library
of
Indiana Classics

BREWSTER'S MILLIONS

George Barr McCutcheon

INDIANA UNIVERSITY PRESS

Bloomington & Indianapolis

This book is a publication of

Indiana University Press
601 North Morton Street
Bloomington, IN 47404-3797 USA

http://www.indiana.edu/~iupress

Telephone orders 800-842-6796
Fax orders 812-855-7931
E-mail orders iuporder@indiana.edu

Brewster's Millions was originally published in 1903 by Herbert S. Stone &
Company. The first Indiana University Press edition, photo-offset from the
1903 edition, was issued in 1999.

The paper used in this publication meets the minimum
requirements of American National Standard for Information
Sciences—Permanence of Paper for Printed Library
Materials, ANSI Z39.48-1984.

Manufactured in the United States of America

George Barr McCutcheon (1866–1928)
Brewster's Millions (originally published under the pseudonym
Richard P. Greaves)

ISBN 0-253-33632-5
ISBN 0-253-21349-5

Library of Congress Cataloging-in-Publication Data

McCutcheon, George Barr, 1866–1928.
　　Brewster's millions / George Barr McCutcheon.
　　　　p. cm. — (Library of Indiana classics)
　　　　　　ISBN 0-253-33632-5 (alk. paper). — ISBN 0-253-21349-5
　　(pbk. : alk. paper)
　　　　I. Title.　II. Series.
　　PS3525.A187B7　1999
　　813'.52—dc21　　　　　　　　　　　　　　　　　99-30003

1 2 3 4 5 04 03 02 01 00 99

CONTENTS

Brewster's Millions

I

"The Little Sons of the Rich" were gathered about the long table in Pettingill's studio. There were nine of them present, besides Brewster. They were all young, more or less enterprising, hopeful, and reasonably sure of better things to come. Most of them bore names that meant something in the story of New York. Indeed one of them had remarked, "A man is known by the street that's named after him," and as he was a new member, they called him "Subway."

The most popular man in the company was young "Monty" Brewster. He was tall and straight and smooth-shaven. People called him "clean-looking." Older women were interested in him because his father and mother had made a romantic runaway match, which was the talk of the town in the seventies, and had never been forgiven. Worldly

women were interested in him because he was
the only grandson of Edwin Peter Brewster,
who was many times a millionaire, and Monty
was fairly certain to be his heir—barring an
absent-minded gift to charity.   Younger
women were interested for a much more obvi-
ous and simple reason: they liked him.   Men
also took to Monty because he was a good
sportsman, a man among men, because he had
a decent respect for himself and no great
aversion to work.

His father and mother had both died while
he was still a child, and, as if to make up for
his long relentlessness, the grandfather had
taken the boy to his own house and had cared
for him with what he called affection.   After
college and some months on the continent,
however, Monty had preferred to be inde-
pendent.   Old Mr. Brewster had found him a
place in the bank, but beyond this and occasional dinners, Monty asked for and received
no favors.   It was a question of work, and
hard work, and small pay.   He lived on his
salary because he had to, but he did not resent
his grandfather's attitude.   He was better satisfied to spend his "weakly salary," as he called
it, in his own way than to earn more by dining
seven nights a week with an old man who had

forgotten he was ever young. It was less wearing, he said.

Among the "Little Sons of the Rich," birthdays were always occasions for feasting. The table was covered with dishes sent up from the French restaurant in the basement. The chairs were pushed back, cigarettes were lighted, men had their knees crossed. Then Pettingill got up.

"Gentlemen," he began, "we are here to celebrate the twenty-fifth birthday of Mr. Montgomery Brewster. I ask you all to join me in drinking to his long life and happiness."

"No heel taps!" some one shouted. "Brewster! Brewster!" all called at once.

"For he's a jolly good fellow,
For he's a jolly good fellow!"

The sudden ringing of an electric bell cut off this flow of sentiment, and so unusual was the interruption that the ten members straightened up as if jerked into position by a string.

"The police!" some one suggested. All faces were turned toward the door. A waiter stood there, uncertain whether to turn the knob or push the bolt.

"Damned nuisance!" said Richard Van Winkle. "I want to hear Brewster's speech."

"Speech!   Speech!" echoed everywhere.
Men settled into their places.

"Mr. Montgomery Brewster," Pettingill
introduced.

Again the bell rang—long and loud.

"Reinforcements.   I'll bet there's a patrol in
the street," remarked Oliver Harrison.

"If it's only the police, let them in," said
Pettingill.   "I thought it was a creditor."

The waiter opened the door.

"Some one to see Mr. Brewster, sir," he
announced.

"Is she pretty, waiter?" called McCloud.

"He says he is Ellis, from your grandfather's,
sir!"

"My compliments to Ellis, and ask him to
inform my grandfather that it's after banking
hours.   I'll see him in the morning," said Mr.
Brewster, who had reddened under the jests of
his companions.

"Grandpa doesn't want his Monty to stay
out after dark," chuckled Subway Smith.

"It was most thoughtful of the old gentleman to have the man call for you with the
perambulator," shouted Pettingill above the
laughter.   "Tell him you've already had your
bottle," added McCloud.

"Waiter, tell Ellis I'm too busy to be seen,"

commanded Brewster, and as Ellis went down in the elevator a roar followed him.

"Now, for Brewster's speech!—Brewster!"

Monty rose.

"Gentlemen, you seem to have forgotten for the moment that I am twenty-five years old this day, and that your remarks have been childish and wholly unbecoming the dignity of my age. That I have arrived at a period of discretion is evident from my choice of friends; that I am entitled to your respect is evident from my grandfather's notorious wealth. You have done me the honor to drink my health and to reassure me as to the inoffensiveness of approaching senility. Now I ask you all to rise and drink to 'The Little Sons of the Rich.' May the Lord love us!"

An hour later "Rip" Van Winkle and Subway Smith were singing "Tell Me, Pretty Maiden," to the uncertain accompaniment of Pettingill's violin, when the electric bell again disturbed the company.

"For Heaven's sake!" shouted Harrison, who had been singing "With All Thy Faults, I Love Thee Still," to Pettingill's lay figure.

"Come home with me, grandson, come home with me now," suggested Subway Smith.

"Tell Ellis to go to Halifax," commanded

Montgomery, and again Ellis took the elevator downward. His usually impassive face now wore a look of anxiety, and twice he started to return to the top floor, shaking his head dubiously. At last he climbed into a hansom and reluctantly left the revelers behind. He knew it was a birthday celebration, and it was only half-past twelve in the morning.

At three o'clock the elevator made another trip to the top floor and Ellis rushed over to the unfriendly doorbell. This time there was stubborn determination in his face. The singing ceased and a roar of laughter followed the hush of a moment or two.

"Come in!" called a hearty voice, and Ellis strode firmly into the studio.

"You are just in time for a 'night-cap,' Ellis," cried Harrison, rushing to the footman's side. Ellis, stolidly facing the young man, lifted his hand.

"No, thank you, sir," he said, respectfully. "Mr. Montgomery, if you'll excuse me for breaking in, I'd like to give you three messages I've brought here to-night."

"You're a faithful old chap," said Subway Smith, thickly. "Hanged if I'd do A. D. T. work till three A. M. for anybody."

"I came at ten, Mr. Montgomery, with a

message from Mr. Brewster, wishing you many happy returns of the day, and with a check from him for one thousand dollars. Here's the check, sir. I'll give my messages in the order I received them, sir, if you please. At twelve-thirty o'clock, I came with a message from Dr. Gower, sir, who had been called in——"

"Called in?" gasped Montgomery, turning white.

"Yes, sir, Mr. Brewster had a sudden heart attack at half-past eleven, sir. The doctor sent word by me, sir, that he was at the point of death. My last message——"

"Good Lord!"

"This time I bring a message from Rawles, the butler, asking you to come to Mr. Brewster's house at once—if you can, sir,—I mean, if you will, sir," Ellis interjected, apologetically. Then with his gaze directed steadily over the heads of the subdued "Sons" he added, impressively:

"Mr. Brewster is dead, sir."

II

SHADES OF ALADDIN

Montgomery Brewster no longer had "prospects." People could not now point him out with the remark that some day he would come into a million or two. He had "realized," as Oliver Harrison would have put it. Two days after his grandfather's funeral a final will and testament was read, and, as was expected, the old banker atoned for the hardships Robert Brewster and his wife had endured by bequeathing one million dollars to their son Montgomery. It was his without a restriction, without an admonition, without an incumbrance. There was not a suggestion as to how it should be handled by the heir. The business training the old man had given him was synonymous with conditions not expressed in the will. The dead man believed that he had drilled into the youth an unmistakable conception of what was expected of him in life; if he failed in these expectations the misfortune would be his alone to bear; a road had been carved out for him and behind him stretched a long line

8

of guide-posts whose laconic instructions might be ignored but never forgotten. Edwin Peter Brewster evidently made his will with the sensible conviction that it was necessary for him to die before anybody else could possess his money, and that, once dead, it would be folly for him to worry over the way in which beneficiaries might choose to manage their own affairs.

The house in Fifth Avenue went to a sister, together with a million or two, and the residue of the estate found kindly disposed relatives who were willing to keep it from going to the Home for Friendless Fortunes. Old Mr. Brewster left his affairs in order. The will nominated Jerome Buskirk as executor, and he was instructed, in conclusion, to turn over to Montgomery Brewster, the day after the will was probated, securities to the amount of one million dollars, provided for in clause four of the instrument. And so it was that on the 26th of September young Mr. Brewster had an unconditional fortune thrust upon him, weighted only with the suggestion of crêpe that clung to it.

Since his grandfather's death he had been staying at the gloomy old Brewster house in Fifth Avenue, paying but two or three hurried visits to the rooms at Mrs. Gray's where he had

made his home. The gloom of death still
darkened the Fifth Avenue place, and there
was a stillness, a gentle stealthiness about
the house that made him long for more cheerful companionship. He wondered dimly if a
fortune always carried the suggestion of tube-
roses. The richness and strangeness of it
all hung about him unpleasantly. He had
had no extravagant affection for the grim
old dictator who was dead, yet his grandfather was a man and had commanded his
respect. It seemed brutal to leave him out of
the reckoning—to dance on the grave of the
mentor who had treated him well. The attitude of the friends who clapped him on the
back, of the newspapers which congratulated
him, of the crowd that expected him to rejoice,
repelled him. It seemed a tragic comedy,
haunted by a severe dead face. He was
haunted, too, by memories, and by a sharp
regret for his own foolish thoughtlessness.
Even the fortune itself weighed upon him at
moments with a half-defined melancholy.

Yet the situation was not without its compensations. For several days when Ellis
called him at seven, he would answer him
and thank fortune that he was not required
at the bank that morning. The luxury of

another hour of sleep seemed the greatest perquisite of wealth. His morning mail amused him at first, for since the newspapers had published his prosperity to the world he was deluged with letters. Requests for public or private charity were abundant, but most of his correspondents were generous and thought only of his own good. For three days he was in a hopeless state of bewilderment. He was visited by reporters, photographers, and ingenious strangers who benevolently offered to invest his money in enterprises with certified futures. When he was not engaged in declining a gold mine in Colorado, worth five million dollars, marked down to four hundred and fifty, he was avoiding a guileless inventor who offered to sacrifice the secrets of a marvelous device for three hundred dollars, or denying the report that he had been tendered the presidency of the First National Bank.

Oliver Harrison stirred him out early one morning and, while the sleepy millionaire was rubbing his eyes and still dodging the bombshell that a dream anarchist had hurled from the pinnacle of a bedpost, urged him in excited, confidential tones to take time by the forelock and prepare for possible breach of promise suits. Brewster sat on the edge of the bed and listened to diabolical stories of how conscienceless females had fleeced innocent and even godly men of wealth. From the bathroom, between splashes, he retained Harrison by the year, month, day and hour, to stand between him and blackmail.

The directors of the bank met and adopted resolutions lamenting the death of their late president, passed the leadership on to the first vice-president and speedily adjourned. The question of admitting Monty to the directory was brought up and discussed, but it was left for Time to settle.

One of the directors was Col. Prentiss Drew, "the railroad magnate" of the newspapers. He had shown a fondness for young Mr. Brewster, and Monty had been a frequent visitor at his house. Colonel Drew called him "my dear boy," and Monty called him "a bully old chap," though not in his presence. But the existence of Miss Barbara Drew may have had something to do with the feeling between the two men.

As he left the directors' room, on the afternoon of the meeting, Colonel Drew came up to Monty who had notified the officers of the bank that he was leaving.

"Ah, my dear boy," said the Colonel, shaking the young man's hand warmly, "now you have a chance to show what you can do. You have a fortune and, with judgment, you ought to be able to triple it. If I can help you in any way, come and see me."

Monty thanked him.

"You'll be bored to death by the raft of people who have ways to spend your money," continued the Colonel. "Don't listen to any of them. Take your time. You'll have a new chance to make money every day of your life, so go slowly. I'd have been rich years and years ago if I'd had sense enough to run away from promoters. They'll all try to get a whack at your money. Keep your eye open, Monty. The rich young man is always a tempting morsel." After a moment's reflection, he added, "Won't you come out and dine with us to-morrow night?"

III

Mrs. Gray lived in Fortieth Street. For years Montgomery Brewster had regarded her quiet, old-fashioned home as his own. The house had once been her grandfather's, and it was one of the pioneers in that part of town. It was there she was born; in its quaint old parlor she was married; and all her girlhood, her brief wedded life, and her widowhood were connected with it. Mrs. Gray and Montgomery's mother had been schoolmates and playmates, and their friendship endured. When old Edwin Peter Brewster looked about for a place to house his orphaned grandson, Mrs. Gray begged him to let her care for the little fellow. He was three years older than her Margaret, and the children grew up as brother and sister. Mr. Brewster was generous in providing for the boy. While he was away at college, spending money in a manner that caused the old gentleman to marvel at his own liberality, Mrs. Gray was well paid for the unused but well-kept apartments, and there never was a murmur of complaint from Edwin

Peter Brewster. He was hard, but he was not niggardly.

It had been something of a struggle for Mrs. Gray to make both ends meet. The property in Fortieth Street was her only possession. But little money had come to her at her husband's death, and an unfortunate speculation of his had swept away all that had fallen to her from her father, the late Judge Merriweather. For years she kept the old home unencumbered, teaching French and English until Margaret was well into her teens. The girl was sent to one of the good old boarding-schools on the Hudson and came out well prepared to help her mother in the battle to keep the wolf down and appearances up. Margaret was rich in friendships; and pride alone stood between her and the advantages they offered. Good-looking, bright, and cheerful, she knew no natural privations. With a heart as light and joyous as a May morning, she faced adversity as though it were a pleasure, and no one would have suspected that even for a moment her courage wavered.

Now that Brewster had come into his splendid fortune he could conceive no greater delight than to share it with them. To walk into the little drawing-room and serenely lay

large sums before them as their own seemed
such a natural proceeding that he refused
to see an obstacle. But he knew it was
there; the proffer of such a gift to Mrs.
Gray would mean a wound to the pride
inherited from haughty generations of men
sufficient unto themselves. There was a small
but troublesome mortgage on the house, a
matter of two or three thousand dollars, and
Brewster tried to evolve a plan by which he
could assume the burden without giving deep
and lasting offense. A hundred wild designs
had come to him, but they were quickly relegated to the growing heap of subterfuges and
pretexts condemned by his tenderness for the
pride of these two women who meant so much
to him.

Leaving the bank, he hastened, by electric
car, to Fortieth Street and Broadway, and then
walked eagerly off into the street of the
numeral. He had not yet come to the point
where he felt like scorning the cars, even
though a roll of banknotes was tucked snugly
away in a pocket that seemed to swell with
sudden affluence. Old Hendrick, faithful serv-
itor through two generations, was sweeping
the autumn leaves from the sidewalk when
Montgomery came up to the house.

"Hello, Hendrick," was the young man's cheery greeting. "Nice lot of leaves you have there."

"So?" ebbed from Hendrick, who did not even so much as look up from his work. Hendrick was a human clam.

"Mrs. Gray in?"

A grunt that signified yes.

"You're as loquacious as ever, Hendrick."

A mere nod.

Brewster let himself in with his own latch key, threw his hat on a chair and unceremoniously bolted into the library. Margaret was seated near a window, a book in her lap. The first evidence of unbiased friendship he had seen in days shone in her smile. She took his hand and said simply, "We are glad to welcome the prodigal to his home again."

"I remind myself more of the fatted calf."

Her first self-consciousness had gone.

"I thought of that, but I didn't dare say it," she laughed. "One must be respectful to rich relatives."

"Hang your rich relatives, Peggy; if I thought that this money would make any difference I would give it up this minute."

"Nonsense, Monty," she said. "How could it make a difference? But you must admit it is rather startling. The friend of our youth leaves his humble dwelling Saturday night with his salary drawn for two weeks ahead. He returns the following Thursday a dazzling millionaire."

"I'm glad I've begun to dazzle, anyway. I thought it might be hard to look the part."

"Well, I can't see that you are much changed." There was a suggestion of a quaver in her voice, and the shadows did not prevent him from seeing the quick mist that flitted across her deep eyes.

"After all, it's easy work being a millionaire," he explained, "when you've always had million-dollar inclinations."

"And fifty-cent possibilities," she added.

"Really though, I'll never get as much joy out of my abundant riches as I did out of financial embarrassments."

"But think how fine it is, Monty, not ever to wonder where your winter's overcoat is to come from and how long the coal will last, and all that."

"Oh, I never wondered about my overcoats; the tailor did the wondering. But I wish I could go on living here just as before. I'd a heap rather live here than at that gloomy place on the avenue."

"That sounded like the things you used to say when we played in the garret. You'd a heap sooner do this than that—don't you remember?"

"That's just why I'd rather live here, Peggy. Last night I fell to thinking of that old garret, and hanged if something didn't come up and stick in my throat so tight that I wanted to cry. How long has it been since we played up there? Yes, and how long has it been since I read 'Oliver Optic' to you, lying there in the garret window while you sat with your back against the wall, your blue eyes as big as dollars?"

"Oh, dear me, Monty, it was ages ago— twelve or thirteen years, at least" she cried, a soft light in her eyes.

"I'm going up there this afternoon to see what the place is like," he said eagerly. "And, Peggy, you must come too. Maybe I can find one of those Optic books, and we'll be young again."

"Just for old time's sake," she said impulsively. "You'll stay for luncheon, too."

"I'll have to be at the—no, I won't, either. Do you know, I was thinking I had to be at the bank at twelve-thirty to let Mr. Perkins go out for something to eat? The millionaire habit

isn't so firmly fixed as I supposed." After a
moment's pause, in which his growing seriousness changed the atmosphere, he went on,
haltingly, uncertain of his position: "The
nicest thing about having all this money is that
—that—we won't have to deny ourselves anything after this." It did not sound very tactful, now that it was out, and he was compelled
to scrutinize rather intently a familiar portrait
in order to maintain an air of careless assurance. She did not respond to this venture, but
he felt that she was looking directly into his
sorely-tried brain. "We'll do any amount of
decorating about the house and—and you know
that furnace has been giving us a lot of trouble
for two or three years—" he was pouring out
ruthlessly, when her hand fell gently on his own
and she stood straight and tall before him, an
odd look in her eyes.

"Don't—please don't go on, Monty," she
said very gently but without wavering. "I
know what you mean. You are good and very
thoughtful, Monty, but you really must not."

"Why, what's mine is yours—" he began

"I know you are generous, Monty, and I
know you have a heart. You want us to—to
take some of your money,"—it was not easy to
say it, and as for Monty, he could only look at

the floor. "We cannot, Monty, dear,—you must never speak of it again. Mamma and I had a feeling that you would do it. But don't you see,—even from you it is an offer of help, and it hurts."

"Don't talk like that, Peggy," he implored.

"It would break her heart if you offered to give her money in that way. She'd hate it, Monty. It is foolish perhaps, but you know we can't take your money."

"I thought you—that you—oh, this knocks all the joy out of it," he burst out desperately.

"Dear Monty!"

"Let's talk it over, Peggy; you don't understand—" he began, dashing at what he thought would be a break in her resolve.

"Don't!" she commanded, and in her blue eyes was the hot flash he had felt once or twice before.

He rose and walked across the floor, back and forth again, and then stood before her, a smile on his lips—a rather pitiful smile, but still a smile. There were tears in her eyes as she looked at him.

"It's a confounded puritanical prejudice, Peggy," he said in futile protest, "and you know it."

"You have not seen the letters that came

for you this morning. They're on the table over there,'' she replied, ignoring him.

He found the letters and resumed his seat in the window, glancing half-heartedly over the contents of the envelopes. The last was from Grant & Ripley, attorneys, and even from his abstraction it brought a surprised "By Jove!" He read it aloud to Margaret.

September 30.

MONTGOMERY BREWSTER, ESQ.,
New York.

Dear Sir:—We are in receipt of a communication from Mr. Swearengen Jones of Montana, conveying the sad intelligence that your uncle, James T. Sedgwick, died on the 24th inst. at M—— Hospital in Portland, after a brief illness. Mr. Jones by this time has qualified in Montana as the executor of your uncle's will and has retained us as his eastern representatives. He incloses a copy of the will, in which you are named as sole heir, with conditions attending. Will you call at our office this afternoon, if it is convenient? It is important that you know the contents of the instrument at once.

Respectfully yours,

GRANT & RIPLEY.

For a moment there was only amazement in the air. Then a faint bewildered smile appeared in Monty's face, and reflected itself in the girl's.

"Who is your Uncle James?" she asked.

"I've never heard of him."

"You must go to Grant & Ripley's at once, of course.'

"Have you forgotten, Peggy," he replied, with a hint of vexation in his voice, "that we are to read 'Oliver Optic' this afternoon?"

IV

A SECOND WILL

"You are both fortunate and unfortunate, Mr. Brewster," said Mr. Grant, after the young man had dropped into a chair in the office of Grant & Ripley the next day. Montgomery wore a slightly bored expression, and it was evident that he took little interest in the will of James T. Sedgwick. From far back in the recesses of memory he now recalled this long-lost brother of his mother. As a very small child he had seen his Uncle James upon the few occasions which brought him to the home of Mr. and Mrs. Robert Brewster. But the young man had dined at the Drews the night before and Barbara had had more charm for him than usual. It was of her that he was thinking when he walked into the office of Swearengen Jones's lawyers.

"The truth is, Mr. Grant, I'd completely forgotten the existence of an uncle," he responded.

"It is not surprising," said Mr. Grant,

genially. "Everyone who knew him in New York nineteen or twenty years ago believed him to be dead. He left the city when you were a very small lad, going to Australia, I think. He was off to seek his fortune, and he needed it pretty badly when he started out. This letter from Mr. Jones comes like a message from the dead. Were it not that we have known Mr. Jones for a long time, handling affairs of considerable importance for him, I should feel inclined to doubt the whole story. It seems that your uncle turned up in Montana about fifteen years ago and there formed a stanch friendship with old Swearengen Jones, one of the richest men in the far West. Sedgwick's will was signed on the day of his death, September 24th, and it was quite natural that Mr. Jones should be named as his executor. That is how we became interested in the matter, Mr. Brewster."

"I see," said Montgomery, somewhat puzzled. "But why do you say that I am both fortunate and unfortunate?"

"The situation is so remarkable that you'll consider that a mild way of putting it when you've heard everything. I think you were told, in our note of yesterday, that you are the sole heir. Well, it may surprise you to learn that James Sedgwick died possessed of an estate valued at almost seven million dollars."

Montgomery Brewster sat like one petrified, staring blankly at the old lawyer, who could say startling things in a level voice.

"He owned gold mines and ranches in the Northwest and there is no question as to their value. Mr. Jones, in his letter to us, briefly outlines the history of James Sedgwick from the time he landed in Montana. He reached there in 1885 from Australia, and he was worth thirty or forty thousand dollars at the time. Within five years he was the owner of a huge ranch, and scarcely had another five years passed before he was part-owner of three rich gold mines. Possessions accumulated rapidly; everything he touched turned to gold. He was shrewd, careful, and thrifty, and his money was handled with all the skill of a Wall Street financier. At the time of his death, in Portland, he did not owe a dollar in the world. His property is absolutely unencumbered— safe and sound as a government bond. It's rather overwhelming, isn't it?" the lawyer concluded, taking note of Brewster's expression.

"And he—he left everything to me?"

"With a proviso."

"Ah!"

"I have a copy of the will. Mr. Ripley and I are the only persons in New York who at present know its contents. You, I am sure, after hearing it, will not divulge them without the most careful deliberation."

Mr. Grant drew the document from a pigeonhole in his desk, adjusted his glasses and prepared to read. Then, as though struck by a sudden thought, he laid the paper down and turned once more to Brewster.

"It seems that Sedgwick never married. Your mother was his sister and his only known relative of close connection. He was a man of most peculiar temperament, but in full possession of all mental faculties. You may find this will to be a strange document, but I think Mr. Jones, the executor, explains any mystery that may be suggested by its terms. While Sedgwick's whereabouts were unknown to his old friends in New York, it seems that he was fully posted on all that was going on here. He knew that you were the only child of your mother and therefore his only nephew. He sets forth the dates of your mother's marriage, of your birth, of the death of Robert Brewster and of Mrs. Brewster. He also was aware of the fact that old Edwin Peter Brewster intended to bequeath a large fortune to you—and thereby hangs a tale. Sedgwick was proud. When he lived in New York, he was regarded as the kind of man who never forgave the person who touched roughly upon his pride. You know, of course, that your father married Miss Sedgwick in the face of the most bitter opposition on the part of Edwin Brewster. The latter refused to recognize her as his daughter, practically disowned his son, and heaped the harshest kind of calumny upon the Sedgwicks. It was commonly believed about town that Jim Sedgwick left the country three or four years after this marriage for the sole reason that he and Edwin Brewster could not live in the same place. So deep was his hatred of the old man that he fled to escape killing him. It was known that upon one occasion he visited the office of his sister's enemy for the purpose of slaying him, but something prevented. He carried that hatred to the grave, as you will see."

Montgomery Brewster was trying to gather himself together from within the fog which made himself and the world unreal.

"I believe I'd like to have you read this extraor—the will, Mr. Grant," he said, with an effort to hold his nerves in leash.

Mr. Grant cleared his throat and began in his still voice. Once he looked up to find his listener eager, and again to find him grown indifferent. He wondered dimly if this were a pose.

In brief, the last will of James T. Sedgwick bequeathed everything, real and personal, of which he died possessed, to his only nephew, Montgomery Brewster of New York, son of Robert and Louise Sedgwick Brewster. Supplementing this all-important clause there was a set of conditions governing the final disposition of the estate. The most extraordinary of these conditions was the one which required the heir to be absolutely penniless upon the twenty-sixth anniversary of his birth, September 23d.

The instrument went into detail in respect to this supreme condition. It set forth that Montgomery Brewster was to have no other worldly possession than the clothes which covered him on the September day named. He was to begin that day without a penny to his name, without a single article of jewelry, furniture or finance that he could call his own or could thereafter reclaim. At nine o'clock, New York time, on the morning of September 23d, the executor, under the provisions of the will,

was to make over and transfer to Montgomery
Brewster all of the moneys, lands, bonds, and
interests mentioned in the inventory which
accompanied the will. In the event that Montgomery Brewster had not, in every particular,
complied with the requirements of the will, to
the full satisfaction of the said executor,
Swearengen Jones, the estate was to be dis-
tributed among certain institutions of charity
designated in the instrument. Underlying
this imperative injunction of James Sedgwick
was plainly discernible the motive that
prompted it. In almost so many words he
declared that his heir should not receive the
fortune if he possessed a single penny that had
come to him, in any shape or form, from the
man he hated, Edwin Peter Brewster. While
Sedgwick could not have known at the time of
his death that the banker had bequeathed one
million dollars to his grandson, it was more
than apparent that he expected the young man
to be enriched liberally by his enemy. It was
to preclude any possible chance of the mingling
of his fortune with the smallest portion of
Edwin P. Brewster's that James Sedgwick, on
his deathbed, put his hand to this astonishing
instrument.

There was also a clause in which he under-

took to dictate the conduct of Montgomery
Brewster during the year leading up to his
twenty-sixth anniversary. He required that
the young man should give satisfactory evi-
dènce to the executor that he was capable of
managing his affairs shrewdly and wisely,—that
he possessed the ability to add to the fortune
through his own enterprise; that he should come
to his twenty-sixth anniversary with a fair name
and a record free from anything worse than
mild forms of dissipation; that his habits be
temperate; that he possess nothing at the end
of the year which might be regarded as a
"visible or invisible asset"; that he make no
endowments; that he give sparingly to charity;
that he neither loan nor give away money, for
fear that it might be restored to him later;
that he live on the principle which inspires a
man to "get his money's worth," be the
expenditure great or small. As these conditions were prescribed for but a single year in
the life of the heir, it was evident that Mr.
Sedgwick did not intend to impose any restrictions after the property had gone into his
hands.

"How do you like it?" asked Mr. Grant, as
he passed the will to Brewster.

The latter took the paper and glanced over

it with the air of one who had heard but had not fully grasped its meaning.

"It must be a joke, Mr. Grant," he said, still groping with difficulty through the fog.

"No, Mr. Brewster, it is absolutely genuine. Here is a telegram from the Probate Court in Sedgwick's home county, received in response to a query from us. It says that the will is to be filed for probate and that Mr. Sedgwick was many times a millionaire. This statement, which he calls an inventory, enumerates his holdings and their value, and the footing shows $6,345,000 in round numbers. The investments, you see, are gilt-edged. There is not a bad penny in all those millions."

"Well, it is rather staggering, isn't it?" said Montgomery, passing his hand over his forehead. He was beginning to comprehend.

"In more ways than one. What are you going to do about it?"

"Do about it?" in surprise. "Why, it's mine, isn't it?"

"It is not yours until next September," the lawyer quietly said.

"Well, I fancy I can wait," said Brewster with a smile that cleared the air.

"But, my dear fellow, you are already the possessor of a million. Do you forget that you are expected to be penniless a year from now?"

"Wouldn't you exchange a million for seven millions, Mr. Grant?"

"But let me inquire how you purpose doing it?" asked Mr. Grant, mildly.

"Why, by the simple process of destruction. Don't you suppose I can get rid of a million in a year? Great Scott, who wouldn't do it! All I have to do is to cut a few purse strings and there is but one natural conclusion. I don't mind being a pauper for a few hours on the 23d of next September."

"That is your plan, then?"

"Of course. First I shall substantiate all that this will sets forth. When I am assured that there can be no possibility of mistake in the extent of this fortune and my undisputed claim, I'll take steps to get rid of my grandfather's million in short order." Brewster's voice rang true now. The zest of life was coming back.

Mr. Grant leaned forward slowly and his intent, penetrating gaze served as a check to the young fellow's enthusiasm.

"I admire and approve the sagacity which urges you to exchange a paltry million for a fortune, but it seems to me that you are forgetting the conditions," he said, slowly. "Has it occurred to you that it will be no easy task to spend a million dollars without in some way violating the restrictions in your uncle's will, thereby losing both fortunes?"

V

A new point of view gradually came to Brewster. All his life had been spent in wondering how to get enough money to pay his bills, and it had not occurred to him that it might be as difficult to spend as to acquire wealth. The thought staggered him for a moment. Then he cried triumphantly, "I can decline to accept grandfather's million."

"You cannot decline to accept what is already yours. I understand that the money has been paid to you by Mr. Buskirk. You have a million dollars, Mr. Brewster, and it cannot be denied."

"You are right," agreed Montgomery, dejectedly. "Really, Mr. Grant, this proposition is too much for me. If you aren't required to give an immediate answer, I want to think it over. It sounds like a dream."

"It is no dream, Mr. Brewster," smiled the lawyer. "You are face to face with an amazing reality. Come in to-morrow morning and see me again. Think it over, study it out.

Remember the conditions of the will and the conditions that confront you. In the meantime, I shall write to Mr. Jones, the executor, and learn from him just what he expects you to do in order to carry out his own conception of the terms of your uncle's will."

"Don't write, Mr. Grant; telegraph. And ask him to wire his reply. A year is not very long in an affair of this kind." A moment later he added, "Damn these family feuds! Why couldn't Uncle James have relented a bit? He brings endless trouble on my innocent head, just because of a row before I was born."

"He was a strange man. As a rule, one does not carry grudges quite so far. But that is neither here nor there. His will is law in this case."

"Suppose I succeed in spending all but a thousand dollars before the 23d of next September! I'd lose the seven millions and be the next thing to a pauper. That wouldn't be quite like getting my money's worth."

"It is a problem, my boy. Think it over very seriously before you come to a decision, one way or the other. In the meantime, we can establish beyond a doubt the accuracy of this inventory."

"By all means, go ahead, and please urge

Mr. Jones not to be too hard on me. I believe I'll risk it if the restrictions are not too severe. But if Jones has puritanical instincts, I might as well give up hope and be satisfied with what I have."

"Mr. Jones is very far from what you'd call puritanical, but he is intensely practical and clear-headed. He will undoubtedly require you to keep an expense account and to show some sort of receipt for every dollar you disburse."

"Good Lord! Itemize?"

"In a general way, I presume."

"I'll have to employ an army of spendthrifts to devise ways and means for profligacy."

"You forget the item which restrains you from taking anybody into your confidence concerning this matter. Think it over. It may not be so difficult after a night's sleep."

"If it isn't too difficult to get the night's sleep."

All the rest of the day Brewster wandered about as one in a dream. He was pre-occupied and puzzled, and more than one of his old associates, receiving a distant nod in passing, resentfully concluded that his wealth was beginning to change him. His brain was so full of statistics, figures, and computations that it whirled dizzily, and once he narrowly

escaped being run down by a cable car. He
dined alone at a small French restaurant in
one of the side streets. The waiter marveled
at the amount of black coffee the young man
consumed and looked hurt when he did not
touch the quail and lettuce.

That night the little table in his room at
Mrs. Gray's was littered with scraps of pad
paper, each covered with an incomprehensible
maze of figures. After dinner he had gone to
his own rooms, forgetting that he lived on
Fifth Avenue. Until long after midnight he
smoked and calculated and dreamed. For the
first time the immensity of that million thrust
itself upon him. If on that very day, October
the first, he were to begin the task of spending
it he would have but three hundred and fifty-
seven days in which to accomplish the end.
Taking the round sum of one million dollars
as a basis, it was an easy matter to calculate
his average daily disbursement. The situation
did not look so utterly impossible until he
held up the little sheet of paper and ruefully
contemplated the result of that simple problem
in mathematics.

It meant an average daily expenditure of
$2,801.12 for nearly a year, and even then there
would be sixteen cents left over, for, in prov-

ing the result of his rough sum in division, he could account for but $999,999.84. Then it occurred to him that his money would be drawing interest at the bank.

"But for each day's $2,801.12, I am getting seven times as much," he soliloquized, as he finally got into bed. "That means $19,607.84 a day, a clear profit of $16,806.72. That's pretty good—yes, too good. I wonder if the bank couldn't oblige me by not charging interest."

The figures kept adding and subtracting themselves as he dozed off, and once during the night he dreamed that Swearengen Jones had sentenced him to eat a million dollars' worth of game and salad at the French restaurant. He awoke with the consciousness that he had cried aloud, "I can do it, but a year is not very long in an affair of this kind."

It was nine o'clock when Brewster finally rose, and after his tub he felt ready to cope with any problem, even a substantial breakfast. A message had come to him from Mr. Grant of Grant & Ripley, announcing the receipt of important dispatches from Montana, and asking him to luncheon at one. He had time to spare, and as Margaret and Mrs. Gray had gone out, he telephoned Ellis to take his horse to the entrance to the park at once. The crisp autumn air was perfect for his ride, and Brewster found a number of smart people already riding and driving in the park. His horse was keen for a canter and he had reached the obelisk before he drew rein. As he was about to cross the carriage road he was nearly run down by Miss Drew in her new French automobile.

"I beg your pardon," she cried. "You're the third person I've run into, so you see I'm not discriminating against you."

"I should be flattered even to be run down by you."

"Very well, then, look out." And she started the machine as if to charge him. She stopped in time, and said with a laugh, "Your gallantry deserves a reward. Wouldn't you rather send your horse home and come for a ride with me?"

"My man is waiting at Fifty-ninth Street. If you'll come that far, I'll go with pleasure."

Monty had merely a society acquaintance with Miss Drew. He had met her at dinners and dances as he had a host of other girls, but she had impressed him more than the others. Something indescribable took place every time their eyes met. Monty had often wondered just what that something meant, but he had always realized that it had in it nothing of platonic affection.

"If I didn't have to meet her eyes," he had said to himself, "I could go on discussing even politics with her, but the moment she looks at me I know she can see what I'm thinking about." From the first they considered themselves very good friends and after their third meeting it seemed perfectly natural that they should call one another by their first names. Monty knew he was treading on dangerous ground. It never occurred to him to wonder what Barbara might think of him. He took it as a matter of course that she must feel more than friendly toward him. As they rode through the maze of carriages, they bowed frequently to friends as they passed. They were conscious that some of the women, noticeably old Miss Dexter, actually turned around and gazed at them.

"Aren't you afraid people will talk about us?" asked Monty with a laugh.

"Talk about our riding together in the park? It's just as safe here as it would be in Fifth Avenue. Besides, who cares? I fancy we can stand it."

"You're a thoroughbred, Barbara. I simply

didn't want you talked about. When I go too far, say the word and drop me.'

"I have a luncheon at two, but until then we have our ride."

Monty gasped and looked at his watch. "Five minutes to one," he cried. The matter of his engagement with the attorney had quite escaped him. In the exhilaration of Miss Drew's companionship he had forgotten even Uncle James's millions.

"I've got a date at one that means life and death to me. Would you mind taking me down to the nearest Elevated—or—here, let me run it."

Almost before Barbara was aware of what was happening they had changed places and the machine, under Monty's guidance, was tearing over the ground.

"Of all the casual people," said the girl, by no means unequal to the excitement, "I believe you're kidnaping me."

But when she saw the grim look on Monty's face and one policeman after another warned him she became seriously alarmed. "Monty Brewster, this pace is positively dangerous."

"Perhaps it is," he responded, "but if they haven't sense enough to keep out of the way, they shouldn't kick if they get run over.''

"I don't mean the people or the automobiles or traps or trees or monuments, Monty; I mean you and me. I know we'll either be killed or arrested.''

"This isn't anything to the gait I'll be going if everything turns out as I expect. Don't be worried, Babs. Besides it's one now. Lord, I didn't dream it was so late.''

"Is your appointment so important?" she asked, hanging on.

"Well, I should say it is, and—look out—you blooming idiot! Do you want to get killed?'' The last remark was hurled back at an indignant pedestrian who had escaped destruction by the merest chance.

"Here we are," he said, as they drew up beside the entrance to the Elevated. "Thanks awfully,—you're a corker,—sorry to leave you this way. I'll tell you all about it later. You're a dear to help me keep my appointment.''

"Seems to me you helped yourself," she cried after him as he darted up the steps. "Come up for tea some day and tell me who the lady is.''

After he had gone Miss Drew turned to her chauffeur who was in the tonneau. Then she laughed unrestrainedly, and the faintest shadow of a grin stole over the man's face.

"Beg pardon, Miss," he said, "but I'd back Mr. Brewster against Fournier any day."

Only half an hour late, Brewster entered the office of Messrs. Grant and Ripley, flushed, eager, and unconscious of the big splotch of mud that decorated his cheek.

"Awfully sorry to have kept you waiting," he apologized.

"Sherlock Holmes would say that you had been driving, Mr. Brewster," said Mr. Ripley, shaking the young man's hand.

"He would miss it, Mr. Ripley. I've been flying. What have you heard from Montana?" He could no longer check the impatient question, which came out so suddenly that the attorneys laughed irresistibly, Brewster joining them an instant later. They laid before him a half dozen telegrams, responses from bankers, lawyers, and mine-operators in Montana. These messages established beyond doubt the extent of James T. Sedgwick's wealth; it was reported to be even greater than shown by the actual figures.

"And what does Mr. Jones say?" demanded Montgomery.

"His reply resembles a press dispatch. He

has tried to make himself thoroughly clear, and if there is anything left unsaid it is past our comprehension. I am sorry to inform you, though, that he has paid the telegraph charges," said Mr. Grant, smiling broadly.

"Is he rational about it?" asked Montgomery, nervously.

Mr. Grant gave his partner a quick, significant glance and then drew from his desk the voluminous telegram from Swearengen Jones. It was as follows:

October 2.

GRANT & RIPLEY,
        Yucatan Building, New York.
    I am to be sole referee in this matter. You are retained as my agents, heir to report to me through you weekly. One desire of uncle was to forestall grandfather's bequest. I shall respect that desire. Enforce terms rigidly. He was my best friend and trusted me with disposition of all this money. Shall attend to it sacredly. Heir must get rid of money left to him in given time. Out of respect to memory of uncle he must take no one into his confidence. Don't want world to think S. was damned fool. He wasn't. Here are rules I want him to work under: 1. No reckless gambling. 2. No idiotic Board of Trade speculation. 3. No endowments to institutions of any character, because their memory would be an invisible asset. 4. No indiscriminate giving away of funds. By that I don't mean him to be stingy. I hate a stingy man and so did J. T. S. 5. No more than

ordinary dissipation.   I hate a saint.   So did J. T. S.
And both of us sowed an oat or two.   6. No excessive
donations to charity.   If he gives as other millionaires
do I'll let it go at that.   Don't believe charity should be
spoiled by indulgence.   It is not easy to spend a million,
and I won't be unreasonable with him.   Let him spend
it freely, but not foolishly, and get his money's worth
out of it.   If he does that I'll consider him a good business man.   I regard it foolish to tip waiter more than
dollar and car porter does not deserve over five.   He
does not earn more than one.   If heir wants to try for
this big stake he'd better begin quick, because he might
slip up if he waits until day of judgment.   It's less
than year off.   Luck to him.   Will write you more fully.

                                                    S. JONES.

"Write more fully!" echoed Montgomery.
"What can there be left to write about?"

"He is explicit," said the attorney, "but it
is best to know all the conditions before you
decide.   Have you made up your mind?"

Brewster sat silent for a long time, staring
hard at the floor.   A great struggle was going
on in his mind.

"It's a gamble, and a big one," he said at
last, squaring his shoulders, "but I'll take it.
I don't want to appear disloyal to my grandfather, but I think that even he would advise
me to accept.   Yes, you may write Mr. Jones
that I accept the chance."

The attorneys complimented him on his

nerve and wished him success. Brewster turned with a smile.

"I'll begin by asking what you think a reasonable fee for an attorney in a case of this kind. I hope you will act for me."

"You don't want to spend it all in a lump, do you?" asked Mr. Grant, smiling. "We can hardly act as counsel for both you and Mr. Jones."

"But I must have a lawyer, and the will limits the number of my confidants. What am I to do?"

"We will consult Mr. Jones in regard to the question. It is not regular, you see, but I apprehend no legal difficulties. We cannot accept fees from both sides, however," said Mr. Grant.

"But I want attorneys who are willing to help me. It won't be a help if you decline to accept my money."

"We'll resort to arbitration," laughed Ripley.

Before night Montgomery Brewster began a career that would have startled the world had the facts been known. With true loyalty to the "Little Sons of the Rich," he asked his friends to dinner and opened their eyes.

"Champagne!" cried Harrison, as they were

seated at table. "I can't remember the last time I had champagne."

"Naturally," laughed "Subway" Smith. "You couldn't remember anything after that."

As the dinner progressed Brewster explained that he intended to double his fortune within a year. "I'm going to have some fun, too," he said, "and you boys are to help me."

"Nopper" Harrison was employed as "superintendent of affairs"; Elon Gardner as financial secretary; Joe Bragdon as private secretary; "Subway" Smith as counsel, and there were places in view for the other members.

"I want the smartest apartment you can find, Nopper," he commanded. "Don't stop at expense. Have Pettingill redecorate it from top to bottom. Get the best servants you can find. I'm going to live, Nopper, and hang the consequences."

VI

A fortnight later Montgomery Brewster had a new home. In strict obedience to his chief's command, "Nopper" Harrison had leased until the September following one of the most expensive apartments to be found in New York City. The rental was $23,000, and the shrewd financial representative had saved $1,000 for his employer by paying the sum in advance. But when he reported this bit of economy to Mr. Brewster he was surprised that it brought forth a frown. "I never saw a man who had less sense about money," muttered "Nopper" to himself. "Why, he spends it like a Chicago millionaire trying to get into New York society. If it were not for the rest of us he'd be a pauper in six months."

Paul Pettingill, to his own intense surprise and, it must be said, consternation, was engaged to redecorate certain rooms according to a plan suggested by the tenant. The rising young artist, in a great flurry of excitement, agreed to do the work for $500, and then

49

blushed like a schoolgirl when he was informed by the practical Brewster that the paints and material for one room alone would cost twice as much.

"Petty, you have no more idea of business than a goat," criticized Montgomery, and Paul lowered his head in humble confession. "That man who calcimines your studio could figure on a piece of work with more intelligence than you reveal. I'll pay $2,500. It's only a fair price, and I can't afford anything cheap in this place."

"At this rate you won't be able to afford anything," said Pettingill to himself.

And so it was that Pettingill and a corps of decorators soon turned the rooms into a confusion of scaffoldings and paint buckets, out of which in the end emerged something very distinguished. No one had ever thought Pettingill deficient in ideas, and this was his opportunity. The only drawback was the time limit which Brewster so remorselessly fixed. Without that he felt that he could have done something splendid in the way of decorative panels—something that would make even the glory of Puvis de Chavannes turn pallid. With it he was obliged to curb his turbulent ideas, and he decided that a rich simplicity was the proper note. The result was gorgeous, but not too gorgeous,—it had depth and distinction.

Elated and eager, he assisted Brewster in selecting furniture and hangings for each room, but he did not know that his employer was making conditional purchases of everything. Mr. Brewster had agreements with all tne dealers to the effect that they were to buy everything back at a fair price, if he desired to give up his establishment within a year. He adhered to this rule in all cases that called for the purchase outright of substantial necessities. The bump of calculativeness in Monty Brewster's head was growing to abnormal proportions.

In retaining his rooms at Mrs. Gray's, he gave the flimsy but pathetic excuse that he wanted a place in which he might find occasional seasons of peace and quiet. When Mrs. Gray protested against this useless bit of extravagance, his grief was so obviously genuine that her heart was touched, and there was a deep, fervent joy in her soul. She loved this fair-faced boy, and tears of happiness came to her eyes when she was given this new proof of his loyalty and devotion. His rooms were kept for him just as if he had expected to occupy them every day and every night, notwithstanding the luxurious apartments he was to maintain elsewhere. The Oliver Optic books still lay in the attic, all tattered and torn, but to Margaret the embodiment of prospective riches, promises of sweet hours to come. She knew Monty well enough to feel that he would not forget the dark little attic of old for all the splendors that might come with the new dispensation.

There was no little surprise when he sent out invitations for a large dinner. His grandfather had been dead less than a month, and society was somewhat scandalized by the plain symptoms of disrespect he was showing. No one had expected him to observe a prolonged season of mourning, but that he should disregard the formalities completely was rather shocking. Some of the older people, who had not long to live and who had heirs-apparent, openly denounced his heartlessness. It was not very gratifying to think of what might be in store for them if all memories were as short as Brewster's. Old Mrs. Ketchell changed her will, and two nephews were cut off entirely; a very modest and impecunious grandson of Joseph Garrity also was to sustain a severe change of fortune in the near future, if the cards spoke correctly. Judge Van Woort, who was not expected to live through the night, got better immediately after hearing some one in the sick-room whisper that Montgomery Brewster was to give a big dinner. Naturally, the heirs-to-be, condemned young Brewster in no uncertain terms.

Nevertheless, the dinner to be given by the grandson of old Edwin Peter Brewster was the talk of the town, and not one of the sixty invited guests could have been persuaded to miss it. Reports as to its magnificence were abroad long before the night set for the dinner. One of them had it that it was to cost $3,000 a plate. From that figure the legendary price receded to a mark as low as $500. Montgomery would have been only too glad to pay $3,000 or more, but some mysterious force conveyed to his mind a perfect portrait of Swearengen Jones in the act of putting down a large black mark against him, and he forbore.

"I wish I knew whether I had to abide by the New York or the Montana standard of extravagance," Brewster said to himself. "I wonder if he ever sees the New York papers."

Late each night the last of the grand old Brewster family went to his bedroom where, after dismissing his man, he settled down at his desk, with a pencil and a pad of paper.

Lighting the candles, which were more easily managed, he found, than lamps, and much more costly, he thoughtfully and religiously calculated his expenses for the day. "Nopper" Harrison and Elon Gardner had the receipts for all moneys spent, and Joe Bragdon was keeping an official report, but the "chief," as they called him, could not go to sleep until he was satisfied in his own mind that he was keeping up the average. For the first two weeks it had been easy—in fact, he seemed to have quite a comfortable lead in the race. He had spent almost $100,000 in the fortnight, but he realized that the greater part of it had gone into the yearly and not the daily expense-account. He kept a "profit and loss" entry in his little private ledger, but it was not like any other account of the kind in the world. What the ordinary merchant would have charged to "loss" he jotted down on the "profit" side, and he was continually looking for opportunities to swell the total.

Rawles, who had been his grandfather's butler since the day after he landed in New York, came over to the grandson's establishment, greatly to the wrath and confusion of the latter's Aunt Emmeline. The chef came from Paris and his name was Detuit. Ellis, the foot-

man, also found a much better berth with Monty
than he had had in the house on the avenue.
Aunt Emmeline never forgave her nephew for
these base and disturbing acts of treachery, as
she called them.

One of Monty's most extraordinary financial
feats grew out of the purchase of a $14,000
automobile. He blandly admitted to "Nopper"
Harrison and the two secretaries that he
intended to use it to practice with only, and
that as soon as he learned how to run an
"auto" as it should be run he expected to buy
a good, sensible, durable machine for $7,000.

His staff officers frequently put their heads
together to devise ways and means of curbing
Monty's reckless extravagance. They were
worried.

"He's like a sailor in port," protested Harrison. "Money is no object if he wants a
thing, and—damn it—he seems to want everything he sees."

"It won't last long," Gardner said, reassur-
ingly. "Like his namesake, Monte Cristo, the
world is his just now and he wants to enjoy it."

"He wants to get rid of it, it seems to me."

Whenever they reproached Brewster about
the matter he disarmed them by saying, "Now
that I've got money I mean to give my friends

a good time.   Just what you'd do if you were
in my place.   What's money for, anyway?"

"But this $3,000-a-plate dinner——"

'I'm going to give a dozen of them, and
even then I can't pay my just debts.   For
years I've been entertained at people's houses
and have been taken cruising on their yachts.
They have always been bully to me, and what
have I ever done for them?   Nothing.   Now
that I can afford it, I am going to return some
of those favors and square myself.   Doesn't it
sound reasonable?"

And so preparations for Monty's dinner
went on.   In addition to what he called his
"efficient corps of gentlemanly aids" he had
secured the services of Mrs. Dan DeMille
as "social mentor and utility chaperon."
Mrs. DeMille was known in the papers as the
leader of the fast younger married set.   She
was one of the cleverest and best-looking young
women in town, and her husband was of
those who did not have to be "invited too."
Mr. DeMille lived at the club and visited his
home.   Some one said that he was so slow and
his wife so fast that when she invited him to
dinner he was usually two or three days late.
Altogether Mrs. DeMille was a decided acquisition to Brewster's campaign committee.   It

required just her touch to make his parties fun instead of funny.

It was on October 18th that the dinner was given. With the skill of a general Mrs. Dan had seated the guests in such a way that from the beginning things went off with zest. Colonel Drew took in Mrs. Valentine and his content was assured; Mr. Van Winkle and the beautiful Miss Valentine were side by side and no one could say he looked unhappy; Mr. Cromwell went in with Mrs. Savage; and the same delicate tact—in some cases it was almost indelicate—was displayed in the disposition of other guests.

Somehow they had come with the expectation of being bored. Curiosity prompted them to accept, but it did not prevent the subsequent inevitable lassitude. Socially Monty Brewster had yet to make himself felt. He and his dinners were something to talk about, but they were accepted hesitatingly, haltingly. People wondered how he had secured the coöperation of Mrs. Dan, but then Mrs. Dan always did go in for a new toy. To her was inevitably attributed whatever success the dinner achieved. And it was no small measure. Yet there was nothing startling about the affair. Monty had decided to begin conserva-

tively.   He did the conventional thing, but he
did it well.   He added a touch or two of
luxury, the faintest aroma of splendor.   Pettingill had designed the curiously wayward
table, with its comfortable atmosphere of companionship, and arranged its decoration of
great lavender orchids and lacy butterfly
festoons of white ones touched with yellow.
He had wanted to use dahlias in their many
rich shades from pale yellow to orange and
deep red, but Monty held out for orchids.   It
was the artist, too, who had found in a rare
and happy moment the massive gold candela-
bra—ancient things of a more luxurious age—
and their opalescent shades.   Against his
advice the service, too, was of gold,—"rank
vulgarity," he called it, with its rich meaning-
less ornamentation.   But here Monty was
obdurate.   He insisted that he liked the color
and that porcelain had no character.   Mrs.
Dan only prevented a quarrel by suggesting that
several courses should be served upon Sèvres.

Pettingill's scheme for lighting the room was
particularly happy.   For the benefit of his
walls and the four lovely Monets which Monty
had purchased at his instigation, he had designed a ceiling screen of heavy rich glass in
tones of white that grew into yellow and dull

green. It served to conceal the lights in the daytime, and at night the glare of electricity was immensely softened and made harmonious by passing through it. It gave a note of quiet to the picture, which caused even these men and women, who had been here and there and seen many things, to draw in their breath sharply. Altogether the effect manifestly made an impression.

Such an environment had its influence upon the company. It went far toward making the dinner a success. From far in the distance came the softened strains of Hungarian music, and never had the little band played the "Valse Amoureuse" and the "Valse Bleue" with the spirit it put into them that night. Yet the soft clamor in the dining-room insistently ignored the emotion of the music. Monty, bored as he was between the two most important dowagers at the feast, wondered dimly what invisible part it played in making things go. He had a vagrant fancy that without it there would have been no zest for talk, no noisy competition to overcome, no hurdles to leap. As it was, the talk certainly went well, and Mrs. Dan inspected the result of her work from time to time with smiling satisfaction. From across the table she heard Colonel Drew's voice,—"Brewster evidently objects to a long siege. He is planning to carry us by assault."

Mrs. Dan turned to "Subway" Smith, who was at her right—the latest addition to her menagerie. "What is this friend of yours?" she asked. "I have never seen such complex simplicity. This new plaything has no real charm for him. He is breaking it to find out what it is made of. And something will happen when he discovers the sawdust."

"Oh, don't worry about him," said "Subway," easily; "Monty's at least a good sportsman. He won't complain, whatever happens. He'll accept the reckoning and pay the piper."

It was only toward the end of the evening that Monty found his reward in a moment with Barbara Drew. He stood before her, squaring his shoulders belligerently to keep away intruders, and she smiled up at him in that bewildering fashion of hers. But it was only for an instant, and then came a terrifying din from the dining-room, followed by the clamor of crashing glass. The guests tried for a moment to be courteously oblivious, but the noise was so startling that such politeness became farcical. The host, with a little laugh, went down the hall. It was the beautiful screen near the ceiling that had fallen. A thousand pieces of shattered glass covered the place. The table was a sickening heap of crushed orchids and sputtering candles. Frightened servants rushed into the room from one side just as Brewster entered from the other. Stupefaction halted them. After the first pulseless moment of horror, exclamations of dismay went up on all sides. For Monty Brewster the first sensation of regret was followed by a diabolical sense of joy.

"Thank the Lord!" he said softly in the hush.

The look of surprise he encountered in the faces of his guests brought him up with a jerk.

"That it didn't happen while we were dining," he added with serene thankfulness. And his nonchalance scored for him in the idle game he was playing.

VII

Mr. Brewster's butler was surprised and annoyed. For the first time in his official career he had unbent so far as to manifest a personal interest in the welfare of his master. He was on the verge of assuming a responsibility which makes any servant intolerable. But after his interview he resolved that he would never again overstep his position. He made sure that it should be the last offense. The day following the dinner Rawles appeared before young Mr. Brewster and indicated by his manner that the call was an important one. Brewster was seated at his writing-table, deep in thought. The exclamation that followed Rawles' cough of announcement was so sharp and so unmistakably fierce that all other evidence paled into insignificance. The butler's interruption came at a moment when Monty's mental arithmetic was pulling itself out of a very bad rut, and the cough drove it back into chaos.

"What is it?" he demanded, irritably.

Rawles had upset his calculations to the extent of seven or eight hundred dollars.

"I came to report h'an h'unfortunate condition h'among the servants, sir," said Rawles, stiffening as his responsibility became more and more weighty. He had relaxed temporarily upon entering the room.

"What's the trouble?"

"The trouble's h'ended, sir."

"Then why bother me about it?"

"I thought it would be well for you to know, sir. The servants was going to ask for 'igher wiges to-day, sir."

"You say they were going to ask? Aren't they?" And Monty's eyes lighted up at the thought of new possibilities.

"I convinced them, sir, as how they were getting good pay as it is, sir, and that they ought to be satisfied. They'd be a long time finding a better place and as good wiges. They 'aven't been with you a week, and here they are strikin' for more pay. Really, sir, these American servants——"

"Rawles, that'll do!" exploded Monty. The butler's chin went up and his cheeks grew redder than ever.

"I beg pardon, sir," he gasped, with a respectful but injured air.

"Rawles, you will kindly not interfere in such matters again. It is not only the privilege, but the duty of every American to strike for higher pay whenever he feels like it, and I want it distinctly understood that I am heartily in favor of their attitude. You will kindly go back and tell them that after a reasonable length of service their wiges—I mean wages—shall be increased. *And don't meddle again*, Rawles."

Late that afternoon Brewster dropped in at Mrs. DeMille's to talk over plans for the next dinner. He realized that in no other way could he squander his money with a better chance of getting its worth than by throwing himself bodily into society. It went easily, and there could be only one asset arising from it in the end—his own sense of disgust.

"So glad to see you, Monty," greeted Mrs. Dan, glowingly, coming in with a rush. "Come upstairs and I'll give you some tea and a cigarette. I'm not at home to anybody."

"That's very good of you, Mrs. Dan," said he, as they mounted the stairs. "I don't know what I'd do without your help." He was thinking how pretty she was.

"You'd be richer, at any rate," turning to smile upon him from the upper landing. "I was in tears half the night, Monty, over that glass screen," she said, after finding a comfortable place among the cushions of a divan. Brewster dropped into a roomy, lazy chair in front of her and handed her a cigarette, as he responded carelessly:

"It amounted to nothing. Of course, it was very annoying that it should happen while the guests were still there." Then he added, gravely, "In strict confidence, I had planned to have it fall just as we were pushing back our chairs, but the confounded thing disappointed me. That's the trouble with these automatic climaxes; they usually hang fire. It was to have been a sort of Fall of Babylon effect, you know."

"Splendid! But like Babylon, it fell at the wrong time."

For a lively quarter of an hour they discussed people about town, liberally approving the slandered and denouncing the slanderers. A still busier quarter of an hour ensued when together they made up the list of dinner guests. He moved a little writing-table up to the divan, and she looked on eagerly while he wrote down the names she suggested after many puckerings of her fair, aristocratic brow, and then drew lines through them when she changed her mind. Mrs. Dan DeMille handled her people without gloves in making up Monty's lists. The dinners were not hers, and she could afford to do as she pleased with his; he was broad and tall and she was not slow to see that he was indifferent. He did not care who the guests were, or how they came; he merely wished to make sure of their presence. His only blunder was the rather diffident recommendation that Barbara Drew be asked again. If he observed that Mrs. Dan's head sank a little closer to the paper, he attached no importance to the movement; he could not see that her eyes grew narrow, and he paid no attention to the little catch in her breath.

"Wouldn't that be a little—just a little pronounced?" she asked, lightly enough.

"You mean—that people might talk?"

"She might feel conspicuously present."

"Do you think so? We are such good friends, you know."

"Of course, if you'd like to have her," slowly and doubtfully, "why, put her name down. But you evidently haven't seen that." Mrs. Dan pointed to a copy of the *Trumpet* which lay on the table.

When he had handed her the paper she

said, " 'The Censor' is growing facetious at your expense."

"I am getting on in society with a vengeance if that ass starts in to write about me. Listen to this"—she had pointed out to him the obnoxious paragraph—" 'If Brewster Drew a diamond flush, do you suppose he'd catch the queen? And if he caught her, how long do you think she'd remain Drew? Or, if she Drew Brewster, would she be willing to learn such a game as Monte?' "

The next morning a writer who signed himself "The Censor" got a thrashing and one Montgomery Brewster had his name in the papers, surrounded by fulsome words of praise.

VIII

THE FORELOCK OF TIME

One morning not long after the incidents just related, Brewster lay in bed, staring at the ceiling, deep in thought. There was a worried pucker on his forehead, half-hidden by the rumpled hair, and his eyes were wide and sleepless. He had dined at the Drew's the evening before and had had an awakening. As he thought of the matter he could recall no special occurrence that he could really use as evidence. Colonel and Mrs. Drew had been as kind as ever and Barbara could not have been more charming. But something had gone wrong and he had endured a wretched evening.

"That little English Johnnie was to blame," he argued. "Of course, Barbara had a right to put any one she liked next to her, but why she should have chosen that silly ass is more than I know. By Jove, if I had been on the other side I'll warrant his grace would have been lost in the dust."

His brain was whirling, and for the first time he was beginning to feel the unpleasant pangs of jealousy. The Duke of Beauchamp he especially disliked, although the poor man had hardly spoken during the dinner. But Monty could not be reconciled. He knew, of course, that Barbara had suitors by the dozen, but it had never occurred to him that they were even seriously considered. Notwithstanding the fact that his encounter with "The Censor" had brought her into undesirable notice, she forgave him everything after a moment's consideration. The first few wrenches of resentment were overbalanced by her American appreciation of chivalry, however inspired. "The Censor" had gone for years unpunished; his coarse wit being aimed at every one who had come into social prominence. So pungent and vindictive was his pen that other men feared him, and there were many who lived in glass houses in terror of a fusilade. Brewster's prompt and sufficient action had checked the pernicious attacks, and he became a hero among men and women. After that night there was no point to "The Censor's" pen. Monty's first qualms of apprehension were swept away when Colonel Drew himself hailed him the morning after the encounter and, in no unmeasured terms, congratulated him upon his achieve-

ment, assuring him that Barbara and Mrs.
Drew approved, although they might lecture
him as a matter of form.

But on this morning, as he lay in his bed,
Monty was thinking deeply and painfully. He
was confronted by a most embarrassing condition and he was discussing it soberly with
himself. "I've never told her," he said to
himself, "but if she doesn't know my feeling
she is not as clever as I think. Besides, I
haven't time to make love to her now. If it
were any other girl I suppose I'd have to, but
Babs, why, she must understand. And yet—
damn that Duke!"

In order to woo her properly he would be
compelled to neglect financial duties that
needed every particle of brain-energy at his
command. He found himself opposed at the
outset by a startling embarrassment, made
absolutely clear by the computations of the
night before. The last four days of indifference to finance on one side, and pampering
the heart on the other, had proved very costly.
To use his own expression, he had been "set
back" almost eight thousand dollars. An
average like that would be ruinous.

"Why, think of it," he continued. "For
each day sacrificed to Barbara I must deduct

something like twenty-five hundred dollars. A long campaign would put me irretrievably in the hole; I'd get so far behind that a holocaust couldn't put me even. She can't expect that of me, yet girls are such idiots about devotion, and of course she doesn't know what a heavy task I'm facing. And there are the others—what will they do while I am out of the running? I cannot go to her and say, 'Please, may I have a year's vacation? I'll come back next September.' On the other hand, I shall surely neglect my business if she expects me to compete. What pleasure shall I get out of the seven millions if I lose her? I can't afford to take chances. That Duke won't have seven millions next September, it's true, but he'll have a prodigious argument against me, about the twenty-first or second."

Then a brilliant thought occurred to him which caused him to ring for a messenger-boy with such a show of impatience that Rawles stood aghast. The telegram which Monty wrote was as follows:

Swearengen Jones,
     Butte, Montana.
   May I marry and turn all property over to wife, providing she will have me?
                Montgomery Brewster.

"Why isn't that reasonable?" he asked himself after the boy had gone. "Making property over to one's wife is neither a loan nor is it charity. Old Jones might call it needless extravagance, since he's a bachelor, but it's generally done because it's good business." Monty was hopeful.

Following his habit in trouble, he sought Margaret Gray, to whom he could always appeal for advice and consolation. She was to come to his next dinner-party, and it was easy to lead up to the subject in hand by mentioning the other guests.

"And Barbara Drew," he concluded, after naming all the others. They were alone in the library, and she was drinking in the details of the dinner as he related them.

"Wasn't she at your first dinner?" she asked, quickly.

He successfully affected mild embarrassment.

"Yes."

"She must be very attractive." There was no venom in Peggy's heart.

"She is attractive. In fact, she's one of the best, Peggy," he said, paving the way.

"It's too bad she seems to care for that little Duke."

"He's a bounder," he argued.

"Well, don't take it to heart. You don't have to marry him," and Peggy laughed.

"But I do take it to heart, Peggy," said Monty, seriously. "I'm pretty hard hit, and I want your help. A sister's advice is always the best in a matter of this sort."

She looked into his eyes dully for an instant, not realizing the full importance of his confession.

"You, Monty?" she said, increduously.

"I've got it bad, Peggy," he replied, staring hard at the floor. She could not understand the cold, gray tone that suddenly enveloped the room. The strange sense of loneliness that came over her was inexplicable. The little something that rose in her throat would not be dislodged, nor could she throw off the weight that seemed pressing down upon her. He saw the odd look in her eyes and the drawn, uncertain smile on her lips, but he attributed them to wonder and incredulity. Somehow, after all these years, he was transformed before her very eyes; she was looking upon a new personality. He was no longer Montgomery, the brother, but she could not explain how and when the change crept over her. What did it all mean? "I am very glad if it will make you happy, Monty," she said slowly, the gray in her lips giving way to red once more. "Does she know?"

"I haven't told her in so many words, Peggy, but—but I'm going to this evening," he announced, lamely.

"This evening?"

"I can't wait," Monty said as he rose to go. "I'm glad you're pleased, Peggy; I need your good wishes. And Peggy," he continued, with a touch of boyish wistfulness, "do you think there's a chance for a fellow? I've had the very deuce of a time over that Englishman."

It was not quite easy for her to say, "Monty, you are the best in the world. Go in and win."

From the window she watched him swing off down the street, wondering if he would turn to wave his hand to her, his custom for years. But the broad back was straight and uncompromising. His long strides carried him swiftly out of sight, but it was many minutes before she turned her eyes, which were smarting, a little from the point where he was lost in the crowd. The room looked ashen to her as she brought her mind back to it, and somehow things had grown difficult.

When Montgomery reached home he found this telegram from Mr. Jones.

MONTGOMERY BREWSTER,
    New York City.
Stick to your knitting, you damned fool.

S. JONES.

IX

It is best not to repeat the expressions Brewster used regarding one S. Jones, after reading his telegram. But he felt considerably relieved after he had uttered them. He fell to reading accounts of the big prize-fight which was to take place in San Francisco that evening. He revelled in the descriptions of "upper cuts" and "left hooks," and learned incidentally that the affair was to be quite one-sided. A local amateur was to box a champion. Quick to see an opportunity, and cajoling himself into the belief that Swearengen Jones could not object to such a display of sportsmanship, Brewster made Harrison book several good wagers on the result. He intimated that he had reason to believe that the favorite would lose. Harrison soon placed three thousand dollars on his man. The young financier felt so sure of the result that he entered the bets on the profit side of his ledger the moment he received Harrison's report.

This done, he telephoned Miss Drew. She was not insensible to the significance of his inquiry if she would be in that afternoon. She had observed in him of late a condition of uneasiness, supplemented by moroseness and occasional periods of irascibility. Every girl whose occupation in life is the study of men recognizes these symptoms and knows how to treat them. Barbara had dealt with many men afflicted in this manner, and the flutter of anticipation that came with his urgent plea to see her was tempered by experience. It had something of joy in it, for she cared enough for Montgomery Brewster to have made her anxiously uncertain of his state of mind. She cared, indeed, much more than she intended to confess at the outset.

It was nearly half past five when he came, and for once the philosophical Miss Drew felt a little irritation. So certain was she of his object in coming that his tardiness was a trifle ruffling. He apologized for being late, and succeeded in banishing the pique that pos· sessed her. It was naturally impossible for him to share all his secrets with her, and that is why he did not tell her that Grant & Ripley had called him up to report the receipt of a telegram from Swearengen Jones, in which the gentleman laconically said he could feed the whole State of Montana for less than six thousand dollars. Beyond that there was no comment. Brewster, in dire trepidation, hastened to the office of the attorneys. They smiled when he burst in upon them.

"Good heavens!" he exclaimed, "does the miserly old hayseed expect me to spend a million for newspapers, cigarettes and Boston terriers? I thought he would be reasonable!"

"He evidently has seen the newspaper accounts of your dinner, and this is merely his comment," said Mr. Ripley.

"It's either a warning, or else he's ambiguous in his compliments," growled Brewster, disgustedly.

"I don't believe he disapproved, Mr. Brewster. In the west the old gentleman is widely known as a wit."

"A wit, eh? Then he'll appreciate an answer from me. Have you a telegraph blank, Mr. Grant?"

Two minutes later the following telegram to Swearengen Jones was awaiting the arrival of a messenger-boy, and Brewster was blandly assuring Messrs. Grant & Ripley that he did not "care a rap for the consequences":

New York, October 23, 1—

Swearengen Jones,
    Butte, Mont.
No doubt you could do it for less than six thousand. Montana is regarded as the best grazing country in the world, but we don't eat that sort of stuff in New York. That's why it costs more to live here.
                    Montgomery Brewster.

Just before leaving his apartments for Miss Drew's home he received this response from far-away Montana:

Butte, Montana, Oct. 23, 1—

Montgomery Brewster,
    New York,
We are eight thousand feet above the level of the sea. I suppose that's why it costs us less to live high.
                    S. Jones.

"I was beginning to despair, Monty," said Miss Drew, reproachfully, when he had come down from the height of his exasperation and remembered that there were things of more importance.

The light in his eyes brought the faintest tinge of red to her cheeks, and where a moment before there had been annoyance there was now a feeling of serenity. For a moment the silence was fraught with purpose. Monty glanced around the room, uncertain how to begin. It was not so easy as he had imagined.

"You are very good to see me," he said at last. "It was absolutely necessary for me to talk to you this evening; I could not have endured the suspense any longer. Barbara, I've spent three or four sleepless nights on your account. Will it spoil your evening if I tell you in plain words what you already know? It won't bother you, will it?" he floundered.

"What do you mean, Monty?" she begged, purposely dense, and with wonderful control of her eyes.

"I love you, Babs," he cried. "I thought you knew about it all along or I should have told you before. That's why I haven't slept. The fear that you may not care for me has driven me nearly to distraction. It couldn't go on any longer. I must know to-day."

There was a gleam in his eyes that made her pose of indifference difficult; the fervor of his half-whispered words took possession of her. She had expected sentiment of such a different character that his frank confession disarmed her completely. Beneath his ardent, abrupt plea there was assurance, the confidence of one who is not to be denied. It was not what he had said, but the way he had said it. A wave of exultation swept over her, tingling through every nerve.

Under the spell her resolution to dally lightly with his emotion suffered a check that almost brought ignominious surrender. Both of her hands were clasped in his when he exultingly resumed the charge against her heart, but she was rapidly regaining control of her emotions and he did not know that he was losing ground with each step he took forward. Barbara Drew loved Brewster, but she was going to make him pay dearly for the brief lapse her composure had experienced. When next she spoke she was again the Miss Drew who had been trained in the ways of the world, and not the young girl in love.

"I care for you a great deal, Monty," she said, "but I'm wondering whether I care enough to—to marry you."

"We haven't known each other very long, Babs," he said, tenderly, "but I think we know each other well enough to be beyond wondering."

"It is like you to manage the whole thing," she said, chidingly. "Can't you give me time to convince myself that I love you as you would like, and as I must love if I expect to be happy with the man I marry?"

"I forgot myself," he said, humbly.

"You forgot me," she protested, gently,

touched by this sign of contrition. "I do care .for you, Monty, but don't you see it's no little thing you ask of me? I must be sure—very sure—before I—before——"

"Don't be so distressed," he pleaded. "You will love me, I know, because you love me now. This means much to me, but it means more to you. You are the woman and you are the one whose happiness should be considered. I can live only in the hope that when I come to you again with this same story and this same question you'll not be afraid to trust yourself to me."

"You deserve to be happy for that, Monty," she said, earnestly, and it was with difficulty that she kept her eyes from wavering as they looked into his.

"You will let me try to make you love me?" he asked, eagerly.

"I may not be worth the struggle."

"I'll take that chance," he replied.

She was conscious of disappointment after he was gone. He had not pleaded as ardently as she had expected and desired, and, try as she would, she could not banish the touch of irrita-tion that had come to haunt her for the night.

Brewster walked to the club, elated that he had at least made a beginning. His position was now clear. Besides losing a fortune he must win Barbara in open competition.

At the theater that evening he met Harrison, who was in a state of jubilation.

"Where did you get that tip?" asked he.

"Tip? What tip?" from Brewster.

"On the prize-fight."

Brewster's face fell and something cold crept over him.

"How did—what was the result?" he asked, sure of the answer.

"Haven't you heard? Your man knocked him out in the fifth round—surprised everybody."

CHAPTER X

The next two months were busy ones for Brewster. Miss Drew saw him quite as often as before the important interview, but he was always a puzzle to her.

"His attitude is changed somehow," she thought to herself, and then she remembered that "a man who wins a girl after an ardent suit is often like one who runs after a street car and then sits down to read his paper."

In truth after the first few days Monty seemed to have forgotten his competitors, and was resting in the consciousness of his assured position. Each day he sent her flowers and considered that he had more than done his duty. He used no small part of his income on the flowers, but in this case his mission was almost forgotten in his love for Barbara.

Monty's attitude was not due to any waning of his affection, but to the very unromantic business in which he was engaged. It seemed to him that, plan as he might, he could not devise fresh ways and means to earn $16,000 a

day. He was still comfortably ahead in the
race, but a famine in opportunities was not far
remote. Ten big dinner parties and a string of
elaborate after-the-play suppers maintained a
fair but insufficient average, and he could see
that the time was ripe for radical measures.
He could not go on forever with his dinners.
People were already beginning to refer to the
fact that he was warming his toes on the Social
Register, and he had no desire to become the
laughing-stock of the town. The few slighting,
sarcastic remarks about his business ability,
chiefly by women and therefore reflected from
the men, hurt him. Miss Drew's apparently
harmless taunt and Mrs. Dan's open criticism told plainly enough how the wind was
blowing, but it was Peggy's gentle questions
that cut the deepest. There was such honest
concern in her voice that he could see how his
profligacy was troubling her and Mrs. Gray.
In their eyes, more than in the others, he felt
ashamed and humiliated. Finally, goaded by
the remark of a bank director which he over-
heard, "Edwin P. Brewster is turning hand-
springs in his grave over the way he is going
it," Monty resolved to redeem himself in the
eyes of his critics. He would show them that
his brain was not wholly given over to frivolity.

With this project in mind he decided to cause a little excitement in Wall Street. For some days he stealthily watched the stock market and plied his friends with questions about values. Constant reading and observation finally convinced him that Lumber and Fuel Common was the one stock in which he could safely plunge. Casting aside all apprehension, so far as Swearengen Jones was concerned, he prepared for what was to be his one and only venture on the Stock Exchange before the 23d of the following September. With all the cunning and craftiness of a general he laid his plans for the attack. Gardner's face was the picture of despair when Brewster asked him to buy heavily in Lumber and Fuel.

"Good heavens, Monty," cried the broker, "you're joking. Lumber is away up now. It can't possibly go a fraction of a point higher. Take my advice and don't touch it. It opened to-day at 111¾ and closed at 109. Why, man, you're crazy to think about it for an instant."

"I know my business, Gardner," said Brewster, quietly, and his conscience smote him when he saw the flush of mortification creep into the face of his friend. The rebuke had cut Gardner to the quick.

"But, Monty, I know what I'm talking

about. At least let me tell you something about this stock," pleaded Elon, loyally, despite the wound.

"Gardy, I've gone into this thing carefully, and if ever a man felt sure about anything I do about this," said Monty, decidedly but affectionately.

"Take my word for it Lumber can't go any higher. Think of the situation; the lumber men in the north and west are overstocked, and there is a strike ready to go into effect. When that comes the stock will go for a song. The slump is liable to begin any day."

"My mind is made up," said the other firmly, and Gardner was in despair. "Will you or will you not execute an order for me at the opening to-morrow? I'll start with ten thousand shares. What will it cost me to margin it for ten points?"

"At least a hundred thousand, exclusive of commission, which would be twelve and a half a hundred shares." Despite the most strenuous opposition from Gardner, Brewster adhered to his design, and the broker executed the order the next morning. He knew that Brewster had but one chance to win, and that was to buy the stock in a lump instead of distributing it among several brokers and throughout

the session.   This was a point that Monty had
overlooked.

There had been little to excite the Stock
Exchange for some weeks; nothing was active
and the slightest flurry was hailed as an
event.   Everyone knew that the calm would be
disturbed at some near day, but nobody looked
for a sensation in Lumber and Fuel.   It was a
foregone conclusion that a slump was coming,
and there was scarcely any trading in the
stock.   When Elon Gardner, acting for Montgomery Brewster took ten thousand shares at
108¾ there was a mighty gasp on the Exchange,
then a rubbing of eyes, then commotion.
Astonishment was followed by nervousness,
and then came the struggle.

Brewster, confident that the stock could go
no higher, and that sooner or later it must
drop, calmly ordered his horse for a ride in the
snow-covered park.   Even though he knew the
venture was to be a failure in the ordinary
sense he found joy in the knowledge that he
was doing something.   He might be a fool,
he was at least no longer inactive.   The feel
of the air was good to him.   He was exhilarated by the 'glitter of the snow, the answering excitement of his horse, the gaiety and
sparkle of life about him.

Somewhere far back in his inner self there seemed to be the sound of cheering and the clapping of hands. Shortly before noon he reached his club, where he was to lunch with Colonel Drew. In the reading-room he observed that men were looking at him in a manner less casual than was customary. Some of them went so far as to smile encouragingly, and others waved their hands in the most cordial fashion. Three or four very young members looked upon him with admiration and envy and even the porters seemed more obsequious. There was something strangely oppressive in all this show of deference.

Colonel Drew's dignity relaxed amazingly when he caught sight of the young man. He came forward to meet him and his greeting almost carried Monty off his feet.

"How did you do it, my boy?" cried the Colonel. "She's off a point or two now, I believe, but half an hour ago she was booming. Gad, I never heard of anything more spectacular!"

Monty's heart was in his mouth as he rushed over to the ticker. It did not take him long to grasp the immensity of the disaster. Gardner had bought in at 108¾, and that very action seemed to put new life into the stock. Just as it was on the point of breaking for lack of support along came this sensational order for ten thousand shares; and there could be but one result. At one time in the morning Lumber and Fuel, traded in by excited holders, touched 113½ and seemed in a fair way to hold firm around that figure.

Other men came up and listened eagerly. Brewster realized that his dash in Lumber and Fuel had been a master-stroke of cleverness when considered from the point of view of these men, but a catastrophe from his own.

"I hope you sold it when it was at the top," said the Colonel anxiously.

"I instructed Gardner to sell only when I gave the word," said Monty, lamely. Several of the men looked at him in surprise and disgust.

"Well, if I were you I'd tell him to sell," remarked the Colonel, coldly.

"The effect of your plunge has worn off, Brewster, and the other side will drive the prices down. They won't be caught napping again, either," said one of the bystanders earnestly.

"Do you think so?" And there was a note of relief in Monty's voice.

From all sides came the advice to sell at

once, but Brewster was not to be pushed. He calmly lighted a cigarette, and with an assured air of wisdom told them to wait a little while and see.

"She's already falling off," said some one at the ticker.

When Brewster's bewildered eyes raced over the figures the stock was quoted at 112. His sigh of relief was heard but misunderstood. He might be saved after all. The stock had started to go down and there seemed no reason why it should stop. As he intended to purchase no more it was fair to assume that the backbone was at the breaking point. The crash was bound to come. He could hardly restrain a cry of joy. Even while he stood at the ticker the little instrument began to tell of a further decline. As the price went down his hopes went up.

The bystanders were beginning to be disgusted. "It was only a fluke after all," they said to each other. Colonel Drew was appealed to to urge Monty to save himself, and he was on the point of remonstrance when the message came that the threatened strike was off, and that the men were willing to arbitrate. Almost before one could draw breath this startling news began to make itself felt. The certainty of a great strike was one of the things that had made Brewster sure that the price could not hold. With this danger removed there was nothing to jeopardize the earning power of the stock. The next quotation was a point higher.

"You sly dog," said the Colonel, digging Monty in the side. "I had confidence in you all the time."

In ten minutes' time Lumber and Fuel was again up to 113 and soaring. Brewster, panic-stricken, rushed to the telephone and called up Gardner.

The broker, hoarse with excitement, was delighted when he recognized Brewster's voice.

"You're a wonder, Monty! I'll see you after the close. How the devil did you do it?" shouted Gardner.

"What's the price now?" asked Brewster.

"One thirteen and three-fourths, and going up all the time. Hooray!"

"Do you think she'll go down again?" demanded Brewster.

"Not if I can help it.

"Very well then, go and sell out," roared Brewster.

"But she's going up like——"

"Sell, damn you! Didn't you hear?"

Gardner, dazed and weak, began selling, and

finally liquidated the full line at prices ranging from 114 to 112½, but Montgomery Brewster had cleared $58,550, and all because it was he and not the market that got excited.

CHAPTER XI

It was not that he had realized heavily in his investments which caused his friends and his enemies to regard him in a new light; his profit had been quite small, as things go on the Exchange in these days. The mere fact that he had shown such foresight proved sufficient cause for the reversal of opinion. Men looked at him with new interest in their eyes, with fresh confidence. His unfortunate operations in the stock market had restored him to favor in all circles. The man, young or old, who could do what he had done with Lumber and Fuel well deserved the new promises that were being made for him.

Brewster bobbed uncertainly between two emotions — elation and distress. He had achieved two kinds of success—the desired and the undesired. It was but natural that he should feel proud of the distinction the venture had brought to him on one hand, but there was reason for despair over the acquisition of $50,000. It made it necessary for him to undertake an almost superhuman feat—increase the number of his January bills. The plans for the ensuing spring and summer were dimly getting into shape and they covered many startling projects. Since confiding some of them to "Nopper" Harrison, that gentleman had worn a never-decreasing look of worry and anxiety in his eyes.

Rawles added to his despair a day or two after the Stock Exchange misfortune. He brought up the information that six splendid little puppies had come to bless his Boston terrier family, and Joe Bragdon, who was present, enthusiastically predicted that he could get $100 apiece for them. Brewster loved dogs, yet for one single horrible moment he longed to massacre the helpless little creatures. But the old affection came back to him, and he hurried out with Bragdon to inspect the brood.

"And I've either got to sell them or kill them," he groaned. Later on he instructed Bragdon to sell the pups for $25 apiece, and went away, ashamed to look their proud mother in the face.

Fortune smiled on him before the day was over, however. He took "Subway" Smith for a ride in the "Green Juggernaut," bad weather and bad roads notwithstanding. Monty lost control of the machine and headed for a subway excavation. He and Smith saved themselves by leaping to the pavement, sustaining slight bruises, but the great machine crashed through the barricade and dropped to the bottom of the trench far below. To Smith's grief and Brewster's delight the automobile was hopelessly ruined, a clear loss of many thousands. Monty's joy was short-lived, for it was soon learned that three luckless workmen down in the depths had been badly injured by the green meteor from above. The mere fact that Brewster could and did pay liberally for the relief of the poor fellows afforded him little consolation. His carelessness, and possibly his indifference, had brought suffering to these men and their families which was not pleasant to look back upon. Lawsuits were avoided by compromises. Each of the injured men received $4,000.

At this time everyone was interested in the charity bazaar at the Astoria. Society was on exhibition, and the public paid for the privilege of gazing at the men and women whose names filled the society columns. Brewster frequented the booth presided over by Miss Drew, and there seemed to be no end to his philanthropy. The bazaar lasted two days and nights, and after that period his account-book showed an even "profit" of nearly $3,000. Monty's serenity, however, was considerably ruffled by the appearance of a new and aggressive claimant for the smiles of the fair Barbara. He was a Californian of immense wealth and unbounded confidence in himself, and letters to people in New York had given him a certain entrée. The triumphs in love and finance that had come with his two score years and ten had demolished every vestige of timidity that may have been born with him. He was successful enough in the world of finance to have become four or five times a millionaire, and he had fared so well in love that twice he had been a widower. Rodney Grimes was starting out to win Barbara with the same dash and impulsiveness that overcame Mary Farrell, the cook in the mining-camp, and Jane Boothroyd, the school-teacher, who came to California ready to marry the first man who asked her. He was a penniless prospector when he married Mary, and when he led Jane to the altar she rejoiced in having captured a husband worth at least $50,000.

He vied with Brewster in patronizing Barbara's booth, and he rushed into the conflict with an impetuosity that seemed destined to carry everything before it. Monty was brushed aside, Barbara was preëmpted as if she were a mining claim and ten days after his arrival in New York, Grimes was the most talked-of man in town. Brewster was not the sort to be dispatched without a struggle, however. Recognizing Grimes as an obstacle, but not as a rival, he once more donned his armor and beset Barbara with all the zest of a champion who seeks to protect and not to conquer. He regarded the Californian as an impostor and summary action was necessary. "I know all about him, Babs," he said one day after he felt sure of his position. "Why, his father was honored by the V. C., on the coast in '49."

"The Victoria Cross?" asked Barbara innocently.

"No, the vigilance committee."

In this way Monty routed the enemy and cleared the field before the end of another week. Grimes transferred his objectionable affection and Barbara was not even asked to be wife number three. Brewster's campaign was so ardent that he neglected other duties deplorably, falling far behind his improvident average. With Grimes disposed of, he once more forsook the battlefield of love and gave his harassed and undivided attention to his own peculiar business.

The fast-and-loose game displeased Miss Barbara greatly. She was at first surprised, then piqued, then resentful. Monty gradually awoke to the distressing fact that she was going to be intractable, as he put it, and forthwith undertook to smooth the troubled sea. To his amazement and concern she was not to be appeased.

"Does it occur to you, Monty," she said, with a gentle coldness that was infinitely worse than heat, "that you have been carrying things with a pretty high hand? Where did you acquire the right to interfere with my privileges? You seem to think that I am not to speak to any man but you."

"O, come now, Babs," retorted Monty, "I've not been quite as unreasonable as that. And you know yourself that Grimes is the worst kind of a bounder."

"I know nothing of the sort," replied the lady, with growing irritation. "You say that about every man who gives me a smile or a flower. Does it indicate such atrocious taste?"

"Don't be silly Barbara. You know perfectly well that you have talked to Gardner and that idiot Valentine by the hour, and I've not said a word. But there are some things I can't stand, and the impertinence of Grimes is one of them.   Jove! he looked at you, out of those fishy eyes, sometimes as though he owned you.   If you knew how many times I've fairly ached to knock him down!"

Inwardly Barbara was weakening a little before his masterfulness.   But she gave no sign.

"And it never occurred to you," she said, with that exasperating coldness of the voice, "that I was equal to the situation.   I suppose you thought Mr. Grimes had only to beckon and I would joyfully answer.   I'll have you know, Monty Brewster, right now, that I am quite able to choose my friends, and to handle them.   Mr. Grimes has character and I like him.   He has seen more of life in a year of his strenuous career than you ever dreamed of in all your pampered existence.   His life has been real, Monty Brewster, and yours is only an imitation."

It struck him hard, but it left him gentle.

"Babs," he said, softly, "I can't take that from you.   You don't really mean it, do you?   Am I as bad as that?"

It was a moment for dominance, and he missed it.   His gentleness left her cold.

"Monty" she exclaimed irritably, "you are terribly exasperating.   Do make up your mind that you and your million are not the only things in the world."

His blood was up now, but it flung him away from her.

"Some day, perhaps, you'll find out that there is not much besides. I am just a little too big, for one thing, to be played with and thrown aside. I won't stand it."

He left the house with his head high in the air, angry red in his cheeks, and a feeling in his heart that she was the most unreasonable of women. Barbara, in the meantime, cried herself to sleep, vowing she would never love Monty Brewster again as long as she lived.

A sharp cutting wind was blowing in Monty's face as he left the house. He was thoroughly wretched.

"Throw up your hands!" came hoarsely from somewhere, and there was no tenderness in the tones. For an instant Monty was dazed and bewildered, but in the next he saw two shadowy figures walking beside him. "Stop where you are, young fellow," was the next command, and he stopped short. He was in a mood to fight, but the sight of a revolver made him think again. Monty was not a coward, neither was he a fool. He was quick to see that a struggle would be madness.

"What do you want?" he demanded as coolly as his nerves would permit.

"Put up your hands quick!" and he hastily obeyed the injunction.

"Not a sound out of you or you get it good and proper. You know what we want. Get to work, Bill; I'll watch his hands."

"Help yourselves, boys. I'm not fool enough to scrap about it. Don't hit me or shoot, that's all. Be quick about it, because I'll take cold if my overcoat is open long. How's business been to-night?" Brewster was to all intents and purposes the calmest man in New York.

"Fierce!" said the one who was doing the searching. "You're the first guy we've seen in a week that looks good."

"I hope you won't be disappointed," said Monty genially. "If I'd expected this I might have brought more money."

"I guess we'll be satisfied," chuckled the man with the revolver. "You're awful nice and kind, mister, and maybe you wouldn't object to tellin' us when you'll be up dis way ag'in."

"It's a pleasure to do business with you, pardner," said the other, dropping Monty's $300 watch in his pocket. "We'll leave car-fare for you for your honesty." His hands were running through Brewster's pockets with the quickness of a machine. "You don't go much on jewelry, I guess. Are dese shoit buttons de real t'ing?"

"They're pearls," said Monty, cheerfully.

"My favorite jool," said the man with the revolver. "Clip 'em out, Bill."

"Don't cut the shirt," urged Monty. "I'm going to a little supper and I don't like the idea of a punctured shirt-front."

"I'll be careful as I kin, mister. There, I guess dat's all. Shall I call a cab for you, sir?"

"No, thank you, I think I'll walk."

"Well, just walk south a hundred steps without lookin' 'round er yellin' and you kin save your skin. I guess you know what I mean, pardner."

"I'm sure I do. Good-night."

"Good-night," came in chuckles from the two hold-up men. But Brewster hesitated, a sharp thought penetrating his mind.

"By gad!" he exclaimed, "you chaps are very careless. Do you know you've missed a roll of three hundred dollars in this overcoat pocket?" The men gasped and the spasmodic oaths that came from them were born of incredulity. It was plain that they doubted their ears.

"Say it ag'in," muttered Bill, in bewildered tones.

"He's stringin' us, Bill," said the other.

"Sure," growled Bill. "It's a nice way to treat us, mister. Move along now and don't turn 'round."

"Well, you're a couple of nice highwaymen," cried Monty in disgust.

"Sh— not so loud."

"That is no way to attend to business. Do you expect me to go down into my pocket and hand you the goods on a silver tray?"

"Keep your hands up! You don't woik dat game on me. You got a gun there."

"No, I haven't. This is on the level. You overlooked a roll of bills in your haste and I'm not the sort of fellow to see an earnest endeavorer get the worst of it My hands are up. See for yourself if I'm not telling you the truth."

"What kind of game is dis?" growled Bill, dazed and bewildered. "I'm blowed if I know w'at to t'ink o' you," cried he in honest amazement. "You don't act drunk, and you ain't crazy, but there's somethin' wrong wid you. Are you givin' it to us straight about de wad?"

"You can find out easily."

"Well, I hate to do it, boss, but I guess we'll just take de overcoat and all. It looks like a trick and we takes no chances. Off wid de coat."

Monty's coat came off in a jiffy and he stood shivering before the dumbfounded robbers.

"We'll leave de coat at de next corner, pardner. It's cold and you need it more'n we do. You're de limit, you are. So long. Walk right straight ahead and don't yell."

Brewster found his coat a few minutes later, and went whistling away into the night. The roll of bills was gone.

CHAPTER XII

Brewster made a good story of the "hold-up" at the club, but he did not relate all the details. One of the listeners was a new public commissioner who was aggressive in his efforts at reform. Accordingly, Brewster was summoned to headquarters the next morning for the purpose of looking over the "suspects" that had been brought in. Almost the first man that he espied was a rough-looking fellow whose identity could not be mistaken. It was Bill.

"Hello, Bill," called Monty, gaily. Bill ground his teeth for a second, but his eyes had such an appeal in them that Monty relented.

"You know this fellow, Mr. Brewster?" demanded the captain, quickly. Bill looked utterly helpless.

"Know Bill?" questioned Monty in surprise. "Of course I do, Captain."

"He was picked up late last night and detained, because he would give no account of his actions."

"Was it as bad as that, Bill?" asked Brewster, with a smile. Bill mumbled something and assumed a look of defiance. Monty's attitude puzzled him sorely. He hardly breathed for an instant, and gulped perceptibly.

"Pass Bill, Captain. He was with me last night just before my money was taken, and he couldn't possibly have robbed me without my knowledge. Wait for me outside, Bill. I want to talk to you. I'm quite sure neither of the thieves is here, Captain," concluded Brewster, after Bill had obeyed the order to step out of the line.

Outside the door the puzzled crook met Brewster, who shook him warmly by the hand.

"You're a peach," whispered Bill, gratefully. "What did you do it for, mister?"

"Because you were kind enough not to cut my shirt."

"Say, you're all right, that's what. Would you mind havin' a drink with me? It's your money, but the drink won't be any the worse for that. We blowed most of it already, but here's what's left." Bill handed Monty a roll of bills.

"I'd a kept it if you'd made a fight," he continued, "but it ain't square to keep it now."

Brewster refused the money, but took back his watch.

"Keep it, Bill," he said, "you need it more than I do. It's enough to set you up in some other trade. Why not try it?"

"I will try, boss," and Bill was so profuse in his thanks that Monty had difficulty in getting away. As he climbed into a cab he heard Bill say, "I will try, boss, and say, if ever I can do anything for you, jes' put me nex'. I'm nex' you all de time."

He gave the driver the name of his club, but as he was passing the Waldorf he remembered that he had several things to say to Mrs. Dan. The order was changed, and a few moments later he was received in Mrs. Dan's very special den. She wore something soft and graceful in lavender, something that was light and wavy and evanescent, and made you watch its changing shadows. Monty looked down at her with the feeling that she made a very effective picture.

"You are looking pretty fit this morning, my lady," he said by way of preamble. "How well everything plays up to you."

"And you are unusually courtly, Monty," she smiled. "Has the world treated you so generously of late?"

"It is treating me generously enough just now to make up for anything," and he looked at her. "Do you know, Mrs. Dan, that it is borne in upon me now and then that there are things that are quite worth while?"

"Oh, if you come to that," she answered, lightly, "everything is worth while. For you, Monty, life is certainly not slow. You can dominate; you can make things go your way. Aren't they going your way now, Monty"— this more seriously—"What's wrong? Is the pace too fast?"

His mood increased upon him with her sympathy. "Oh, no," he said, "it isn't that. You are good—and I'm a selfish beast. Things are perverse and people are desperately obstinate sometimes. And here I'm taking it out on you. You are not perverse. You are not obstinate. You are a ripper, Mrs. Dan, and you are going to help me out in more ways than one."

"Well, to pay for all these gallantries, Monty, I ought to do much. I'm your friend through thick and thin. You have only to command me."

"It was precisely to get your help that I came in. I'm tired of those confounded dinners. You know yourself that they are all alike—the same people, the same flowers, the same things to eat, and the same inane twaddle in the shape of talk. Who cares about them anyway?"

"Well, I like that," she interrupted. "After all the thought I put into those dinners, after all the variety I so carefully secured! My dear boy, you are frightfully ungrateful."

"Oh, you know what I mean And you know quite as well as I do that it is perfectly true. The dinners were a beastly bore, which proves that they were a loud success. Your work was not done in vain. But now I want something else. We must push along this ball we've been talking of. And the yachting cruise—that can't wait very much longer."

"The ball first," she decreed. "I'll see to the cards at once, and in a day or two I'll have a list ready for your gracious approval. And what have you done?"

"Pettingill has some great ideas for doing over Sherry's. Harrison is in communication with the manager of that Hungarian orchestra you spoke of, and he finds the men quite ready for a little jaunt across the water. We have that military band—I've forgotten the number of its regiment—for the promenade music, and the new Paris sensation, the contralto, is coming over with her primo tenore for some special numbers.''

''You were certainly cut out for an executive, Monty,'' said Mrs. Dan. ''But with the music and the decorations arranged, you've only begun. The favors are the real thing, and if you say the word, we'll surprise them a little. Don't worry about it. Monty. It's a go already. We'll pull it off together.''

''You are a thoroughbred, Mrs Dan,'' he exclaimed. ''You do help a fellow at a pinch.''

''That's all right, Monty,'' she answered; ''give me until after Christmas and I'll have the finest favors ever seen. Other people may have their paper hats and pink ribbons but you can show them how the thing ought to be done.

Her reference to Christmas haunted Brewster, as he drove down Fifth Avenue, with the dread of a new disaster. Never before had he looked upon presents as a calamity; but this year it was different. Immediately he began to plan a bombardment of his friends with costly trinkets, when he grew suddenly doubtful of the opinion of his uncle's executor upon this move. But in response to a telegram, Swearengen Jones, with pleasing irascibility, informed him that ''anyone with a drop of human kindness in his body would consider it his duty to give Christmas presents to those who deserved them." Monty's way was now clear. If his friends meant to handicap him with gifts, he knew a way to get even. For two weeks his mornings were spent at Tiffany's, and the afternoons brought joy to the heart of every dealer in antiquities in Fourth and Fifth Avenues. He gave much thought to the matter in the effort to secure many small articles which elaborately concealed their value. And he had taste. The result of his endeavor was that many friends who would not have thought of remembering Monty with even a card were pleasantly surprised on Christmas Eve.

As it turned out, he fared very well in the matter of gifts, and for some days much of his time was spent in reading notes of profuse thanks, which were yet vaguely apologetic. The Grays and Mrs. Dan had remembered him with an agreeable lack of ostentation, and some of the "Little Sons of the Rich," who had kept one evening a fortnight open for the purpose of "using up their meal-tickets" at Monty's, were only too generously grateful. Miss Drew had forgotten him, and when they met after the holiday her recognition was of the coldest. He had thought that, under the circumstances, he could send her a gift of value, but the beautiful pearls with which he asked for a reconciliation were returned with "Miss Drew's thanks."   He loved Barbara sincerely, and it cut.   Peggy Gray was taken into his confidence and he was comforted by her encouragement.   It was a bit difficult for her to advise him to try again, but his happiness was a thing she had at heart.

"It's beastly unfair, Peggy," he said.   "I've really been white to her.   I believe I'll chuck the whole business and leave New York."

"You're going away?" and there was just a suggestion of a catch in her breath.

"I'm going to charter a yacht and sail away from this place for three or four months." Peggy fairly gasped.   "What do you think of the scheme?" he added, noticing the alarm and incredulity in her eyes.

"I think you'll end in the poor-house, Montgomery Brewster," she said, with a laugh.

CHAPTER XIII

A FRIEND IN NEED

It was while Brewster was in the depths of despair that his financial affairs had a windfall. One of the banks in which his money was, deposited failed and his balance of over $100,000 was wiped out. Mismanagement was the cause and the collapse came on Friday, the thirteenth day of the month. Needless to say it destroyed every vestige of the superstition he may have had regarding Friday and the number thirteen.

Brewster had money deposited in five banks, a transaction inspired by the wild hope that one of them might some day suspend operations and thereby prove a legitimate benefit to him. There seemed no prospect that the bank could resume operations, and if the depositors in the end realized twenty cents on the dollar they would be fortunate. Notwithstanding the fact that everybody had considered the institution substantial there were not a few wiseacres who called Brewster a fool and were so unreasonable as to say that he did not know how to handle money. He heard that Miss Drew, in particular, was bitterly sarcastic in referring to his stupidity.

This failure caused a tremendous flurry in banking circles. It was but natural that questions concerning the stability of other banks should be asked, and it was not long before many wild, disquieting reports were afloat. Anxious depositors rushed into the big banking institutions and then rushed out again, partially assured that there was no danger. The newspapers sought to allay the fears of the people, but there were many to whom fear became panic. There were short, wild runs on some of the smaller banks, but all were in a fair way to restore confidence when out came the rumor that the Bank of Manhattan Island was in trouble. Colonel Prentiss Drew, railroad magnate, was the president of this bank.

When the bank opened for business on the Tuesday following the failure, there was a stampede of frightened depositors. Before eleven o'clock the run had assumed ugly proportions and no amount of argument could stay the onslaught. Colonel Drew and the directors, at first mildly distressed, and then seeing that the affair had become serious, grew more alarmed than they could afford to let the public

see. The loans of all of the banks were
unusually large. Incipient runs on some had
put all of them in an attitude of caution and
there was a natural reluctance to expose their
own interests to jeopardy by coming to the
relief of the Bank of Manhattan Island.

Monty Brewster had something like $200,000
in Colonel Drew's bank. He would not have
regretted on his own account the collapse of
this institution, but he realized what it meant
to the hundreds of other depositors, and for
the first time he appreciated what his money
could accomplish. Thinking that his presence
might give confidence to the other depositors
and stop the run he went over to the bank with
Harrison and Bragdon. The tellers were
handing out thousands of dollars to the eager
depositors. His friends advised him strongly
to withdraw before it was too late, but Monty
was obdurate. They set it down to his desire
to help Barbara's father and admired his
nerve.

"I understand, Monty," said Bragdon, and
both he and Harrison went among the people
carelessly asking one another if Brewster had
come to withdraw his money. "No, he has
over $200,000, and he's going to leave it," the
other would say.

Each excited group was visited in turn by the two men, but their assurance seemed to accomplish but little. These men and women were there to save their fortunes; the situation was desperate.

Colonel Drew, outwardly calm and serene, but inwardly perturbed, finally saw Brewster and his companions. He sent a messenger over with the request that Monty come to the president's private office at once.

"He wants to help you to save your money," cried Bragdon in low tones. "That shows it's all up."

"Get out every dollar of it, Monty, and don't waste a minute. It's a smash as sure as fate," urged Harrison, a feverish expression in his eyes.

Brewster was admitted to the Colonel's private office. Drew was alone and was pacing the floor like a caged animal.

"Sit down, Brewster, and don't mind if I seem nervous. Of course we can hold out, but it is terrible—terrible. They think we are trying to rob them. They're mad—utterly mad."

"I never saw anything like it, Colonel. Are you sure you can meet all the demands?" asked Brewster, thoroughly excited. The Colonel's face was white and he chewed his cigar nervously.

"We can hold out unless some of our heaviest depositors get the fever and swoop down upon us. I appreciate your feelings in an affair of this kind, coming so swiftly upon the heels of the other, but I want to give you my personal assurance that the money you have here is safe. I called you in to impress you with the security of the bank. You ought to know the truth, however, and I will tell you in confidence that another check like Austin's, which we paid a few minutes ago, would cause us serious, though temporary, embarrassment."

"I came to assure you that I have not thought of withdrawing my deposits from this bank, Colonel. You need have no uneasiness——"

The door opened suddenly and one of the officials of the bank bolted inside, his face as white as death. He started to speak before he saw Brewster, and then closed his lips despairingly.

"What is it, Mr. Moore?" asked Drew, as calmly as possible. "Don't mind Mr. Brewster."

"Oglethorp wants to draw two hundred and

fifty thousand dollars," said Moore in strained tones.

"Well, he can have it, can't he?" asked the Colonel quietly. Moore looked helplessly at the president of the bank, and his silence spoke more plainly than words.

"Brewster, it looks bad," said the Colonel, turning abruptly to the young man. The other banks are afraid of a run and we can't count on much help from them. Some of them have helped us and others have refused. Now, I not only ask you to refrain from drawing out your deposit, but I want you to help us in this crucial moment." The Colonel looked twenty years older and his voice shook perceptibly. Brewster's pity went out to him in a flash.

"What can I do, Colonel Drew?" he cried. "I'll not take my money out, but I don't know how I can be of further assistance to you. Command me, sir."

"You can restore absolute confidence, Monty, my dear boy, by increasing your deposits in our bank," said the Colonel slowly, and as if dreading the fate of the suggestion.

"You mean, sir, that I can save the bank by drawing my money from other banks and putting it here?" asked Monty, slowly. He was thinking harder and faster than he had ever thought in his life. Could he afford to risk the loss of his entire fortune on the fate of this bank? What would Swearengen Jones say if he deliberately deposited a vast amount of money in a tottering institution like the Bank of Manhattan Island? It would be the maddest folly on his part if the bank went down. There could be no mitigating circumstances in the eyes of either Jones or the world, if he swamped all of his money in this crisis.

"I beg of you, Monty, help us." The Colonel's pride was gone. "It means disgrace if we close our doors even for an hour; it means a stain that only years can remove. You can restore confidence by a dozen strokes of your pen, and you can save us."

He was Barbara's father. The proud old man was before him as a suppliant, no longer the cold man of the world. Back to Brewster's mind came the thought of his quarrel with Barbara and of her heartlessness. A scratch of the pen, one way or the other, could change the life of Barbara Drew. The two bankers stood by scarcely breathing. From outside came the shuffle of many feet and the muffled roll of voices. Again the door to the private office opened and a clerk excitedly motioned

for Mr. Moore to hurry to the front of the
bank.   Moore paused irresolutely, his eyes
on Brewster's face.   The young man knew the
time had come when he must help or deny
them.

Like a flash the situation was made clear to
him and his duty was plain.   He remembered
that the Bank of Manhattan Island held every
dollar that Mrs. Gray and Peggy possessed;
their meager fortune had been entrusted to the
care of Prentiss Drew and his associates, and it
was in danger.

"I will do all I can, Colonel," said Monty,
"but upon one condition."

"That is?"

"Barbara must never know of this."   The
Colonel's gasp of astonishment was cut short
as Monty continued.   "Promise that she shall
never know."

"I don't understand, but if it is your wish I
promise."

Inside of half an hour's time several hundred
thousand came to the relief of the struggling
bank, and the man who had come to watch the
run with curious eyes turned out to be its
savior.   His money won the day for the Bank
of Manhattan Island.   When the happy president and directors offered to pay him an

astonishingly high rate of interest for the use of the money he proudly declined.

The next day Miss Drew issued invitations for a cotillion. Mr. Montgomery Brewster was not asked to attend.

CHAPTER XIV

Miss Drew's cotillion was not graced by the presence of Montgomery Brewster. It is true he received an eleventh-hour invitation and a very cold and difficult little note of apology, but he maintained heroically the air of disdain that had succeeded the first sharp pangs of disappointment. Colonel Drew, in whose good graces Monty had firmly established himself, was not quite guiltless of usurping the rôle of dictator in the effort to patch up a truce. A few nights before the cotillion, when Barbara told him that Herbert Alling was to lead, he explosively expressed surprise. "Why. not Monty Brewster, Babs?" he demanded.

"Mr. Brewster is not coming," she responded calmly.

"Going to be out of town?"

"I'm sure I do not know," stiffly.

"What's this?"

"He has not been asked, father." Miss Drew was not in good humor.

"Not asked?" said the Colonel in amazement. "It's ridiculous, Babs, send him an invitation at once."

"This is my dance, father, and I don't want to ask Mr. Brewster."

The Colonel sank back in his chair and struggled to overcome his anger. He knew that Barbara had inherited his willfulness, and had long since discovered that it was best to treat her with tact.

"I thought you and he were—"but the Colonel's supply of tact was exhausted.

"We were"—in a moment of absent mindedness. "But it's all over," said Barbara.

"Why, child, there wouldn't have been a cotillion if it hadn't been for—" but the Colonel remembered his promise to Monty and checked himself just in time. "I—I mean there will not be any party, if Montgomery Brewster is not asked. That is all I care to say on the subject," and he stamped out of the room.

Barbara wept copiously after her father had gone, but she realized that his will was law and that Monty must be invited. "I will send an invitation," she said to herself, "but if Mr. Brewster comes after he has read it, I shall be surprised."

Montgomery, however, did not receive the note in the spirit in which it had been sent. He only saw in it a ray of hope that Barbara was relenting and was jubilant at the prospect of a reconciliation. The next Sunday he sought an interview with Miss Drew, but she received him with icy reserve. If he had thought to punish her by staying away, it was evident that she felt equally responsible for a great deal of misery on his part. Both had been more or less unhappy, and both were resentfully obstinate. Brewster felt hurt and insulted, while she felt that he had imposed upon her disgracefully. He was now ready to cry quits and it surprised him to find her obdurate. If he had expected to dictate the terms of peace he was woefully disappointed when she treated his advances with cool contempt.

"Barbara, you know I care very much for you," he was pleading, fairly on the road to submission. "I am sure you are not quite indifferent to me. This foolish misunderstanding must really be as disagreeable to you as it is to me."

"Indeed," she replied, lifting her brows disdainfully. "You are assuming a good deal, Mr. Brewster."

"I am merely recalling the fact that you once told me you cared. You would not promise anything, I know, but it meant much that you cared. A little difference could not have changed your feeling completely."

"When you are ready to treat me with respect I may listen to your petition," she said, rising haughtily.

"My petition?" He did not like the word and his tact quite deserted him. "It's as much yours as mine. Don't throw the burden of responsibility on me, Miss Drew."

"Have I suggested going back to the old relations? You will pardon me if I remind you of the fact that you came to-day on your own initiative and certainly without my solicitation."

"Now, look here, Barbara—" he began, dimly realizing that it was going to be hard, very hard, to bring her to reason.

"I am very sorry, Mr. Brewster, but you will have to excuse me. I am going out."

"I regret exceedingly that I should have disturbed you to-day, Miss Drew," he said swallowing his pride. "Perhaps I may have the pleasure of seeing you again."

As he was leaving the house, deep anger in his soul, he encountered the Colonel. There was something about Monty's greeting, cordial as it was, that gave the older man a hint as to the situation.

"Won't you stop for dinner, Monty?" he asked, in the hope that his suspicion was groundless.

"Thank you, Colonel, not to-night," and he was off before the Colonel could hold him.

Barbara was tearfully angry when her father came into the room, but as he began to remonstrate with her the tears disappeared and left her at white heat.

"Frankly, father, you don't understand matters," she said with slow emphasis; "I wish you to know now that if Montgomery Brewster calls again, I shall not see him."

"If that is your point of view, Barbara, I wish you to know mine." The Colonel rose and stood over her, everything forgotten but the rage that went so deep that it left the surface calm. Throwing aside his promise to Brewster, he told Barbara with dramatic simplicity the story of the rescue of the bank. "You see," he added, "if it had not been for that open-hearted boy we would now be ruined. Instead of giving cotillions, you might be giving music lessons. Montgomery Brewster will always be welcome in this house and you will see that my wishes are respected. Do you understand?"

"Perfectly," Barbara answered in a still voice. "As your friend I shall try to be civil to him."

The Colonel was not satisfied with so cold-blooded an acquiescence, but he wisely retired from the field. He left the girl silent and crushed, but with a gleam in her eyes that was not altogether to be concealed. The story had touched her more deeply than she would willingly confess. It was something to know that Monty Brewster could do a thing like that, and would do it for her. The exultant smile which it brought to her lips could only be made to disappear by reminding herself sharply of his recent arrogance. Her anger, she found, was a plant which needed careful cultivation.

It was in a somewhat chastened mood that she started a few days later for a dinner at the DeMille's. As she entered in her sweeping golden gown the sight of Monty Brewster at the other end of the room gave her a flutter at the heart. But it was an agitation that was very carefully concealed. Brewster was certainly unconscious of it. To him the position of guest was like a disguise and he was pleased at the prospect of letting himself go under the mask without responsibility. But it took on a different color when the butler handed him a card which signified that he was to take Miss Drew in to dinner. Hastily seeking out the hostess he endeavored to convey to her the impossibility of the situation.

"I hope you won't misunderstand me," he said. "But is it too late to change my place at the table?"

"It isn't conventional, I know, Monty. Society's chief aim is to separate engaged couples at dinner," said Mrs. Dan with a laugh. "It would be positively compromising if a man and his wife sat together."

Dinner was announced before Monty could utter another word, and as she led him over to Barbara she said, "Behold a generous hostess who gives up the best man in the crowd so that he and someone else may have a happy time. I leave it to you, Barbara, if that isn't the test of friendship."

For a moment the two riveted their eyes on the floor. Then the humor of the situation came to Monty.

"I did not know that we were supposed to do Gibson tableaux to-night," he said drily as he proffered his arm.

"I don't understand," and Barbara's curiosity overcame her determination not to speak.

"Don't you remember the picture of the man who was called upon to take his late fiancée out to dinner?"

The awful silence with which this remark was received put an end to further efforts at humor.

The dinner was probably the most painful experience in their lives. Barbara had come to it softened and ready to meet him half way. The right kind of humility in Monty would have found her plastic. But she had very definite and rigid ideas of his duty in the premises. And Monty was too simple minded to seem to suffer, and much too flippant to understand. It was plain to each that the other did not expect to talk, but they both realized that they owed a duty to appearances and to their hostess. Through two courses, at least, there was dead silence between them. It seemed as though every eye in the room were on them and every mind were speculating. At last, in sheer desperation, Barbara turned to him with the first smile he had seen on her face in days. There was no smile in her eyes, however, and Monty understood.

"We might at least give out the impression that we are friends," she said quietly.

"More easily said than done," he responded gloomily.

"They are all looking at us and wondering."

"I don't blame them."

"We owe something to Mrs. Dan, I think."

"I know."

Barbara uttered some inanity whenever she caught anyone looking in their direction, but Brewster seemed not to hear. At length he cut short some remark of hers about the weather.

"What nonsense this is, Barbara," he said. "With anyone else I would chuck the whole game, but with you it is different. I don't know what I have done, but I am sorry. I hope you'll forgive me."

"Your assurance is amusing, to say the least."

"But I am sure. I know this quarrel is something we'll laugh over. You keep forgetting that we are going to be married some-day."

A new light came into Barbara's eyes. "You forget that my consent may be necessary," she said.

"You will be perfectly willing when the time

comes. I am still in the fight and eventually you will come to my way of thinking."

"Oh! I see it now," said Barbara, and her blood was up. "You mean to force me to it. What you did for father—"

Brewster glowered at her, thinking that he had misunderstood. "What do you mean?" he said.

"He has told me all about that wretched bank business. But poor father thought you quite disinterested. He did not see the little game behind your melodrama. He would have torn up your check on the instant if he had suspected you were trying to buy his daughter."

"Does your father believe that?" asked Brewster.

"No, but I see it all now. His persistence and yours—you were not slow to grasp the opportunity he offered."

"Stop, Miss Drew," Monty commanded. His voice had changed and she had never before seen that look in his eyes. "You need have no fear that I will trouble you again."

CHAPTER XV

THE CUT DIRECT

A typographical error in one of the papers caused no end of amusement to every one except Monty and Miss Drew. The headlines had announced: "Magnificent ball to be given Miss Drew by her Finance," and the "Little Sons of the Rich" wondered why Monty did not see the humor of it.

"He has too bad an attack to see anything but the lady," said Harrison one evening when the "Sons" were gathered for an old-time supper party.

"It's always the way," commented the philosophical Bragdon. "When you lose your heart your sense of humor goes too. Engaged couples couldn't do such ridiculous stunts if they had the least particle of it left."

"Well if Monty Brewster is still in love with Miss Drew he takes a mighty poor way of showing it." "Subway" Smith's remark fell like a bombshell. The thought had come to everyone, but no one had been given the courage to utter it. For them Brewster's silence on the subject since the DeMille dinner seemed to have something ominous behind it.

"It's probably only a lover's quarrel," said Bragdon. But further comment was cut short by the entrance of Monty himself, and they took their places at table.

Before the evening came to an end they were in possession of many astonishing details in connection with the coming ball. Monty did not say that it was to be given for Miss Drew and her name was conspicuously absent from his descriptions. As he unfolded his plans even the "Little Sons," who were imaginative by instinct and reckless on principle, could not be quite acquiescent.

"Nopper" Harrison solemnly expressed the opinion that the ball would cost Brewster at least $125,000. The "Little Sons" looked at one another in consternation, while Brewster's indifference expressed itself in an unflattering comment upon his friend's vulgarity. "Good Lord, Nopper," he added; "you would speculate about the price of gloves for your wedding."

Harrison resented the taunt. "It would be much less vulgar to do that, Monty, saving your presence, than to force your millions down everyone's throat."

"Well, they swallow them, I've noticed," retorted Brewster, "as though they were chocolates."

Pettingill interrupted grandiloquently. "My friends and gentlemen!"

"Which is which?" asked Van Winkle, casually.

But the artist was in the saddle. "Permit me to present you to the boy Crœsus—the only one extant. His marbles are plunks and his kites are made of fifty-dollar notes. He feeds upon coupons à la Newburgh, and his champagne is liquid golden eagles. Look at him, gentlemen, while you can, and watch him while he spends thirteen thousand dollars for flowers!"

"With a Viennese orchestra for twenty-nine thousand!" added Bragdon. "And yet they maintain that silence is golden."

"And three singers to divide twelve thousand among themselves! That's absolutely criminal," cried Van Winkle. "Over in Germany they'd sing a month for half that amount."

"Six hundred guests to feed—total cost of not less than forty thousand dollars," groaned "Nopper," dolefully.

"And there aren't six hundred in town,"

lamented "Subway" Smith. "All that glory wasted on two hundred rank outsiders."

"You men are borrowing a lot of trouble," yawned Brewster with a gallant effort to seem bored. "All I ask of you is to come to the party and put up a good imitation of having the time of your life. Between you and me I'd rather be caught at Huyler's drinking ice cream soda than giving this thing. But—"

"That's what we want to know, but what?" and "Subway" leaned forward eagerly.

"But," continued Monty, "I am in for it now, and it is going to be a ball that is a ball."

Nevertheless the optimistic Brewster could not find the courage to tell Peggy of these picturesque extravagances. To satisfy her curiosity he blandly informed her that he was getting off much more cheaply than he had expected. He laughingly denounced as untrue the stories that had come to her from outside sources. And before his convincing assertions that reports were ridiculously exaggerated, the troubled expression in the girl's eyes disappeared.

"I must seem a fool," groaned Monty, as he left the house after one of these explanatory trials, "but what will she think of me toward the end of the year when I am really in harness.'' He found it hard to control the desire to be straight with Peggy and tell her the story of his mad race in pursuit of poverty.

Preparations for the ball went on steadily, and in a dull winter it had its color value for society. It was to be a Spanish costume-ball, and at many tea-tables the talk of it was a god-send. Sarcastic as it frequently was on the question of Monty's extravagance, there was a splendor about the Aladdin-like entertainment which had a charm. Beneath the outward disapproval there was a secret admiration of the superb nerve of the man. And there was little reluctance to help him in the wild career he had chosen. It was so easy to go with him to the edge of the precipice and let him take the plunge alone. Only the echo of the criticism reached Brewster, for he had silenced Harrison with work and Pettingill with opportunities. It troubled him little, as he was engaged in jotting down items that swelled the profit side of his ledger account enormously. The ball was bound to give him a good lead in the race once more, despite the heavy handicap the Stock Exchange had imposed. The ''Little Sons'' took off their coats and helped

Pettingill in the work of preparation. He found them quite superfluous, for their ideas never agreed and each man had a way of preferring his own suggestion. To Brewster's chagrin they were united in the effort to curb his extravagance.

"He'll be giving automobiles and ropes of pearls for favors if we don't stop him," said "Subway" Smith, after Monty had ordered a vintage champagne to be served during the entire evening. "Give them two glasses first, if you like, and then they won't mind if they have cider the rest of the night."

"Monty is plain dotty," chimed in Bragdon, "and the pace is beginning to tell on him."

As a matter of fact the pace was beginning to tell on Brewster. Work and worry were plainly having an effect on his health. His color was bad, his eyes were losing their lustre, and there was a listlessness in his actions that even determined effort could not conceal from his friends. Little fits of fever annoyed him occasionally and he admitted that he did not feel quite right.

"Something is wrong somewhere," he said, ruefully, "and my whole system seems ready to stop work through sympathy."

Suddenly there was a mighty check to the

preparations. Two days before the date set for the ball everything came to a standstill and the managers sank back in perplexity and consternation. Monty Brewster was critically ill.

Appendicitis, the doctors called it, and an operation was imperative.

"Thank heaven it's fashionable," laughed Monty, who showed no fear of the prospect. "How ridiculous if it had been the mumps, or if the newspapers had said, 'On account of the whooping-cough, Mr. Brewster did not attend his ball.' "

"You don't mean to say—the ball is off, of course," and Harrison was really alarmed.

"Not a bit of it, Nopper," said Monty. "It's what I've been wanting all along. You chaps do the handshaking and I stay at home."

There was an immediate council of war when this piece of news was announced, and the "Little Sons" were unanimous in favor of recalling the invitations and declaring the party off. At first Monty was obdurate, but when some one suggested that he could give the ball later on, after he was well, he relented. The opportunity to double the cost by giving two parties was not to be ignored.

"Call it off, then, but say that it is only postponed."

A great rushing to and fro resulted in the cancelling of contracts, the recalling of invitations, the settling of accounts, with the most loyal effort to save as much as possible from the wreckage. Harrison and his associates, almost frantic with fear for Brewster's life, managed to perform wonders in the few hours of grace. Gardner, with rare foresight, saw that the Viennese orchestra would prove a dead loss. He suggested the possibility of a concert tour through the country, covering several weeks, and Monty, too ill to care one way or the other, authorized him to carry out the plan if it seemed feasible.

To Monty, fearless and less disturbed than any other member of his circle, appendicitis seemed as inevitable as vaccination.

"The appendix is becoming an important feature in the Book of Life," he once told Peggy Gray.

He refused to go to a hospital, but pathetically begged to be taken to his old rooms at Mrs. Gray's.

With all the unhappy loneliness of a sick boy, he craved the care and companionship of those who seemed a part of his own. Dr Lotless had them transform a small bedchamber into a model operating room and Monty took no small satisfaction in the thought that if he was to be denied the privilege of spending money for several weeks, he would at least make his illness as expensive as possible. A consultation of eminent surgeons was called, but true to his colors, Brewster installed Dr. Lotless, a "Little Son," as his house surgeon. Monty grimly bore the pain and suffering and submitted to the operation which alone could save his life. Then came the struggle, then the promise of victory and then the quiet days of convalescence. In the little room where he had dreamed his boyish dreams and suffered his boyish sorrows, he struggled against death and gradually emerged from the mists of lassitude. He found it harder than he had thought to come back to life. The burden of it all seemed heavy. The trained nurses found that some more powerful stimulant than the medicine was needed to awaken his ambition, and they discovered it at last in Peggy.

"Child," he said to her the first time she was permitted to see him, and his eyes had lights in them; "do you know, this isn't such a bad old world after all. Sometimes as I've lain here, it has looked twisted and queer. But there are things that straighten it out. To-day I feel as though I had a place in it—as though I could fight things and win out. What do you think, Peggy? Do you suppose there is something that I could do? You know what I mean—something that some one else would not do a thousand times better."

But Peggy, to whom this chastened mood in Monty was infinitely pathetic, would not let him talk. She soothed him and cheered him and touched his hair with her cool hands. And then she left him to think and brood and dream.

It was many days before his turbulent mind drifted to the subject of money, but suddenly he found himself hoping that the surgeons would be generous with their charges. He almost suffered a relapse when Lotless, visibly distressed, informed him that the total amount would reach three thousand dollars.

"And what is the additional charge for the operation?" asked Monty, unwilling to accept such unwarranted favors.

"It's included in the three thousand," said Lotless. They knew you were my friend and it was professional etiquette to help keep down expenses."

For days Brewster remained at Mrs. Gray's, happy in its restfulness, serene under the charm of Peggy's presence, and satisfied to be hopelessly behind in his daily expense account. The interest shown by the inquiries at the house and the anxiety of his friends were soothing to the profligate. It gave him back a little of his lost self-respect. The doctors finally decided that he would best recuperate in Florida, and advised a month at least in the warmth. He leaped at the proposition, but took the law into his own hands by ordering General Manager Harrison to rent a place, and insisting that he needed the companionship of Peggy and Mrs. Gray.

"How soon can I get back to work, Doctor?" demanded Monty, the day before the special train was to carry him south. He was beginning to see the dark side of this enforced idleness. His blood again was tingling with the desire to be back in the harness of a spendthrift.

"To work?" laughed the physician. "And what is your occupation, pray?"

"Making other people rich," responded Brewster, soberly.

"Well, aren't you satisfied with what you have done for me? If you are as charitable as that you must be still pretty sick. Be careful, and you may be on your feet again in five or six weeks."

Harrison came in as Lotless left. Peggy smiled at him from the window. She had been reading aloud from a novel so garrulous that it fairly cried aloud for interruptions.

"Now, Nopper, what became of the ball I was going to give?" demanded Monty, a troubled look in his eyes.

"Why, we called it off," said "Nopper," in surprise.

"Don't you remember, Monty?" asked Peggy, looking up quickly, and wondering if his mind had gone trailing off.

"I know we didn't give it, of course; but what date did you hit upon?"

"We didn't postpone it at all," said "Nopper." How could we? We didn't know whether —I mean, it wouldn't have been quite right to do that sort of thing."

"I understand. Well, what has become of the orchestra, and the flowers, and all that?"

"The orchestra is gallivanting around the country, quarreling with itself and everybody else, and driving poor Gardner to the insane asylum. The flowers have lost their bloom long ago."

"Well, we'll get together, Nopper, and try to have the ball at mid-Lent. I think I'll be well by that time."

Peggy looked appealingly at Harrison for guidance, but to him silence seemed the better part of valor, and he went off wondering if the illness had completely carried away Monty's reason.

CHAPTER XVI

It was the cottage of a New York millionaire which had fallen to Brewster. The owner had, for the time, preferred Italy to St. Augustine, and left his estate, which was well located and lavishly equipped, in the hands of his friends. Brewster's lease covered three months, at a fabulous rate per month. With Joe Bragdon installed as manager-in-chief, his establishment was tranferred bodily from New York, and the rooms were soon as comfortable as their grandeur would permit. Brewster was not allowed to take advantage of his horses and the new automobile which preceded him from NewYork, but to his guests they offered unlimited opportunities. "Nopper" Harrison had remained in the north to renew arrangements for the now hated ball and to look after the advance details of the yacht cruise. Dr. Lotless and his sister, with "Subway" Smith and the Grays, made up Brewster's party. Lotless dampened Monty's spirits by relentlessly putting him on rigid diet, with most discouraging restrictions upon his conduct. The period of convalescence was to be an exceedingly trying one for the invalid. At first he was kept in door, and the hours were whiled away by playing cards. But Monty considered "bridge" the "pons asinorum," and preferred to play piquet with Peggy. It was one of these games that the girl interrupted with a question that had troubled her for many days. "Monty," she said, and she found it much more difficult than when she had rehearsed the scene in the silence of her walks; "I've heard a rumor that Miss Drew and her mother have taken rooms at the hotel. Wouldn't it be pleasanter to have them here?"

A heavy gloom settled upon Brewster's face, and the girl's heart dropped like lead. She had puzzled over the estrangement, and wondered if by any effort of her own things could be set right. At times she had had flashing hopes that it did not mean as much to Monty as she had thought. But down underneath, the fear that he was unhappy seemed the only certain thing in life. She felt that she must make sure. And together with the very human desire to know the worst, was the puritanical impulse to bring it about.

"You forget that this is the last place they

would care to invade." And in Brewster's
face Peggy seemed to read that for her martyr-
dom was the only wear. Bravely she put it on.

"Monty, I forget nothing that I really know.
But this is a case in which you are quite wrong.
Where is your sporting blood? You have
never fought a losing fight before, and you
can't do it now. You have lost your nerve,
Monty. Don't you see that this is the time
for an aggressive campaign?" Somehow she
was not saying things at all as she had planned
to say them. And his gloom weighed heavily
upon her. "You don't mind, do you, Monty,"
she added, more softly, "this sort of thing from
me? I know I ought not to interfere, but I've
known you so long. And I hate to see things
twisted by a very little mistake."

But Monty did mind enormously. He had
no desire to talk about the thing anyway, and
Peggy's anxiety to marry him off seemed a bit
unnecessary. Manifestly her own interest in
him was of the coldest. From out of the
gloom he looked at her somewhat sullenly.
For the moment she was thinking only of his
pain, and her face said nothing.

"Peggy," he exclaimed, finally, resenting
the necessity of answering her, "you don't in
the least know what you are talking about. It

is not a fit of anger on Barbara Drew's part. It is a serious conviction."

"A conviction which can be changed," the girl broke in.

"Not at all." Brewster took it up. "She has no faith in me. She thinks I'm an ass."

"Perhaps she's right," she exclaimed, a little hot. "Perhaps you have never discovered that girls say many things to hide their emotions. Perhaps you don't realize what feverish, exclamatory, foolish things girls are. They don't know how to be honest with the men they love, and they wouldn't if they did. You are little short of an idiot, Monty Brewster, if you believed the things she said rather than the things she looked."

And Peggy, fiery and determined and defiantly unhappy, threw down her cards and escaped so that she might not prove herself tearfully feminine. She left Brewster still heavily enveloped in melancholy; but she left him puzzled. He began to wonder if Barbara Drew did have something in the back of her mind. Then he found his thoughts wandering off toward Peggy and her defiance. He had only twice before seen her in that mood, and he liked it. He remembered how she had lost her temper once when she was fifteen, and

hated a girl he admired. Suddenly he laughed
aloud at the thought of the fierce little picture
she had made, and the gloom, which had been
so sedulously cultivated, was dissipated in a
moment. The laugh surprised the man who
brought in some letters. One of them was
from "Nopper" Harrison, and gave him all
the private news. The ball was to be given at
mid-Lent, which arrived toward the end of
March, and negotiations were well under way
for the chartering of the "Flitter," the steam-
yacht belonging to Reginald Brown, late of
Brown & Brown.

The letter made Brewster chafe under the
bonds of inaction. His affairs were getting
into a discouraging state. The illness was certain to entail a loss of more than $50,000 to his
business. His only consolation came through
Harrison's synopsis of the reports from Gardner, who was managing the brief American tour
of the Viennese orchestra. Quarrels and dissen-
sions were becoming every-day embarrassments, and the venture was an utter failure
from a financial point of view. Broken contracts and lawsuits were turning the tour into
one continuous round of losses, and poor
Gardner was on the point of despair. From the
beginning, apparently, the concerts had been

marked for disaster. Public indifference had aroused the scorn of the irascible members of the orchestra, and there was imminent danger of a collapse in the organization. Gardner lived in constant fear that his troop of quarrelsome Hungarians would finish their tour suddenly in a pitched battle with daggers and steins. Brewster smiled at the thought of the practical Gardner trying to smooth down the electric emotions of these musicians.

A few days later Mrs. Prentiss Drew and Miss Drew registered at the Ponce de Leon, and there was much speculation upon the chances for a reconciliation. Monty, however, maintained a strict silence on the subject, and refused to satisfy the curiosity of his friends. Mrs. Drew had brought down a small crowd, including two pretty Kentucky girls and a young Chicago millionaire. She lived well and sensibly, and with none of the extravagance that characterized the cottage. Yet it was inevitable that Brewster's guests should see hers and join some of their riding parties. Monty pleaded that he was not well enough to be in these evcursions, but neither he nor Barbara cared to over-emphasize their estrangement.

Peggy Gray was in despair over Monty's atti-

tude.   She had become convinced that behind
his pride he was cherishing a secret longing for
Barbara.   Yet she could not see how the walls
were to be broken down if he maintained this
icy reserve.   She was sure that the masterful
tone was the one to win with a girl like that,
but evidently Monty would not accept advice.
That he was mistaken about Barbara's feeling
she did not doubt for a moment, and she saw
things going hopelessly wrong for want of a
word.   There were times when she let herself
dream of possibilities, but they always ended
by seeming too impossible. She cared too much
to make the attainment of her vision seem simple.   She cared too much to be sure of anything.

At moments she fancied that she might say
a word to Miss Drew which would straighten
things out.   But there was something about
her which held her off.   Even now that they
were thrown together more or less she could
not get beyond a certain barrier. It was not
until a sunny day when she had accepted Barbara's invitation to drive that things seemed to
go more easily.   For the first time she felt the
charm of the girl, and for the first time Barbara
seemed unreservedly friendly.   It was a quiet
drive they were taking through the woods

and out along the beach, and somehow in the open air things simplified themselves. Finally, in the softness and the idle warmth, even an allusion to Monty, whose name usually meant an embarrassing change of subject, began to seem possible. It was inevitable that Peggy should bring it in; for with her a question of tact was never allowed to dominate when things of moment were at stake. She cowered before the plunge, but she took it unafraid.

"The doctor says Monty may go out driving tomorrow," she began. "Isn't that fine?"

Barbara's only response was to touch her pony a little too sharply with the whip. Peggy went on as if unconscious of the challenge.

"He has been bored to death, poor fellow, in the house all this time, and —"

"Miss Gray, please do not mention Mr. Brewster's name to me again," interrupted Barbara, with a contraction of the eyebrows. But Peggy was seized with a spirit of defiance and plunged recklessly on.

"What is the use, Miss Drew, of taking an attitude like that? I know the situation pretty well, and I can't believe that either Monty or you has lost in a week a feeling that was so deep-seated. I know Monty much too well to think that he would change so easily." Peggy still lived largely in her ideals. "And you are too fine a thing not to have suffered under this misunderstanding. It seems as if a very small word would set you both straight."

Barbara drew herself up and kept her eyes on the road which lay white and gleaming in the sun. "I have not the least desire to be set straight." And she was never more serious.

"But it was only a few weeks ago that you were engaged."

"I am sorry," answered Barbara, "that it should have been talked about so much. Mr. Brewster did ask me to marry him, but I never accepted. In fact, it was only his persistence that made me consider the matter at all. I did think about it. I confess that I rather liked him. But it was not long before I found him out."

"What do you mean?" And there was a flash in Peggy's eyes. "What has he done?"

"To my certain knowledge he has spent more than four hundred thousand dollars since last September. That is something, is it not?" Miss Drew said, in her slow, cool voice, and even Peggy's loyalty admitted some justification in the criticism.

"Generosity has ceased to be a virtue then?" she asked coldly.

"Generosity!" exclaimed Barbara, sharply. "It's sheer idiocy. Haven't you heard the things people are saying? They are calling him a fool, and in the clubs they are betting that he will be a pauper within a year."

"Yet they charitably help him to spend his money. And I have noticed that even worldly mammas find him eligible." The comment was not without its caustic side.

"That was months ago, my dear," protested Barbara, calmly. "When he spoke to me— he told me it would be impossible for him to marry within a year. And don't you see that a year may make him an abject beggar?"

"Naturally anything is preferable to a beggar," came in Peggy's clear, soft voice.

Barbara hesitated only a moment.

"Well, you must admit, Miss Gray, that it shows a shameful lack of character. How could any girl be happy with a man like that? And, after all, one must look out for one's own fate."

"Undoubtedly," replied Peggy, but many thoughts were dashing through her brain.

"Shall we turn back to the cottage?" she said, after an awkward silence.

"You certainly don't approve of Mr. Brewster's conduct?" Barbara did not like to be placed in the wrong, and felt that she must endeavor to justify herself. "He is the most reckless of spendthrifts, we know, and he probably indulges in even less respectable excitement."

Peggy was not tall, but she carried her head at this moment as though she were in the habit of looking down on the world.

"Aren't you going a little too far, Miss Drew?" she asked placidly.

"It is not only New York that laughs over his Quixotic transactions," Barbara persisted. "Mr. Hampton, our guest from Chicago, says the stories are worse out there than they are in the east."

"It is a pity that Monty's illness should have made him so weak," said Peggy quietly, as they turned in through the great iron gates, and Barbara was not slow to see the point.

CHAPTER XVII

THE NEW TENDERFOOT

Brewster was comparatively well and strong when he returned to New York in March. His illness had interfered extensively with his plan of campaign and it was imperative that he redouble his efforts, notwithstanding the manifest dismay of his friends. His first act was to call upon Grant & Ripley, from whom he hoped to learn what Swearengen Jones thought of his methods. The lawyers had heard no complaint from Montana, and advised him to continue as he had begun, assuring him, as far as they could, that Jones would not prove unreasonable.

An exchange of telegrams just before his operation had renewed Monty's dread of his eccentric mentor.

New York, Jan. 6, 19—

SWEARENGEN JONES,
         Butte, Mont.

How about having my life insured? Would it violate conditions?

MONTGOMERY BREWSTER.

To Montgomery Brewster,
                    New York.
    Seems to me your life would become an asset in that
case.   Can you dispose of it before September 23d?
                                              Jones.

To Swearengen Jones,
                    Butte, Mont.
    On the contrary I think life will be a debt by that
time.   Montgomery Brewster.

To Montgomery Brewster,
                    New York.
    If you feel that way about it, I advise you to take out
a $500 policy.   Jones.

To Swearengen Jones,
                    Butte, Mont.
    Do you think that amount would cover funeral
expenses?   Montgomery Brewster.

To Montgomery Brewster,
                    New York.
    You won't be caring about expenses if it comes to that.
                                              Jones.

The invitations for the second ball had been
out for some time and the preparations were
nearly complete when Brewster arrived upon
the scene of festivity.   It did not surprise him
that several old-time friends should hunt him
up and protest vigorously against the course he

was pursuing. Nor did it surprise him when he found that his presence was not as essential to the success of some other affair as it had once been. He was not greeted as cordially as before, and he grimly wondered how many of his friends would stand true to the end. The uncertainty made him turn more and more often to the unquestioned loyalty of Peggy Gray, and her little library saw him more frequently than for months.

Much as he had dreaded the pretentious and resplendent ball, it was useful to him in one way at least. The "profit" side of his ledger account was enlarged and in that there was room for secret satisfaction. The Viennese orchestra straggled into New York, headed by Elon Gardner, a physical wreck, in time to make a harmonious farewell appearance behind Brewster's palms, which caused his guests to wonder why the American public could not appreciate the real thing. A careful summing up of the expenses and receipts proved that the tour had been a bonanza for Brewster. The net loss was a trifle more than $56,000. When this story became known about town, everybody laughed pityingly, and poor Gardner was almost in tears when he tried to explain the disaster to the man who lost the money. But Monty's sense of humor, singularly enough, did not desert him on this trying occasion.

Æsthetically the ball proved to be the talk of more than one season. Pettingill had justified his desire for authority and made a name which would last. He had taken matters into his own hands while Brewster was in Florida, and changed the period from the Spain of Velasquez to France and Louis Quinze. After the cards were out he remembered, to his consternation, that the favors purchased for the Spanish ball would be entirely inappropriate for the French one. He wired Brewster at once of this misfortune, and was astonished at the nonchalance of his reply. "But then Monty always was a good sort," he thought, with a glow of affection. The new plan was more costly than the old, for it was no simple matter to build a Versailles suite at Sherry's. Pettingill was no imitator, but he created an effect which was superbly in keeping with the period he had chosen. Against it the rich costumes, with their accompaniment of wigs and powdered hair, shone out resplendent. With great difficulty the artist had secured for Monty a costume in white satin and gold brocade, which might once have adorned the person of Louis himself. It made him feel like a popinjay, and it was with infinite relief that he took it off an hour or so after dawn. He knew that things had gone well, that even Mrs. Dan was satisfied; but the whole affair made him heartsick. Behind the compliments lavished upon him he detected a note of irony, which revealed the laughter that went on behind his back. He had not realized how much it would hurt. "For two cents," he thought, "I'd give up the game and be satisfied with what's left." But he reflected that such a course would offer no chance to redeem himself. Once again he took up the challenge and determined to win out. "Then," he thought exultantly, "I'll make them feel this a bit."

He longed for the time when he could take his few friends with him and sail away to the Mediterranean to escape the eyes and tongues of New York. Impatiently he urged Harrison to complete the arrangements, so that they could start at once. But Harrison's face was not untroubled when he made his report. All the preliminary details had been perfected. He had taken the "Flitter" for four months, and it was being overhauled and put into condition for the voyage. It had been Brown's special pride, but at his death it went to heirs who were ready and eager to rent it to the highest bidder. It would not have been easy to find a handsomer yacht in New York waters. A picked crew of fifty men were under command of Captain Abner Perry. The steward was a famous manager and could be relied upon to stock the larder in princely fashion. The boat would be in readiness to sail by the tenth of April.

"I think you are going in too heavily, Monty," protested Harrison, twisting his fingers nervously. "I can't for my life figure how you can get out for less than a fortune, if we do everything you have in mind. Wouldn't it be better to pull up a bit? This looks like sheer madness. You won't have a dollar, Monty—honestly you won't."

"It's not in me to save money, Nopper, but if you can pull out a few dollars for yourself I shall not object."

"You told me that once before, Monty," said Harrison, as he walked to the window. When he resolutely turned back again to Brewster his face was white, but there was a look of determination around the mouth.

"Monty, I've got to give up this job," he said, huskily. Brewster looked up quickly.

"What do you mean, Nopper?"

"I've got to leave, that's all," said Harrison, standing stiff and straight and looking over Brewster's head

"Good Lord, Nopper, I can't have that. You must not desert the ship. What's the matter, old chap? You're as white as a ghost. What is it?" Monty was standing now and his hands were on Harrison's shoulders, but before the intensity of his look, his friend's eyes fell helplessly.

"The truth is, Monty, I've taken some of your money and I've lost it. That's the reason I—I can't stay on. I have betrayed your confidence."

"Tell me about it," and Monty was perhaps more uncomfortable than his friend. "I don't understand."

"You believed too much in me, Monty. You see, I thought I was doing you a favor. You were spending so much and getting nothing in return, and I thought I saw a chance to help you out. It went wrong, that's all, and before I could let go of the stock sixty thousand dollars of your money had gone. I can't replace it yet. But God knows I didn't mean to steal."

"It's all right, Nopper. I see that you thought you were helping me. The money's gone and that ends it. Don't take it so hard, old boy."

"I knew you'd act this way, but it doesn't help matters. Some day I may be able to pay back the money I took, and I'm going to work until I do."

Brewster protested that he had no use for the money and begged him to retain the position of trust he had held. But Harrison had too much self-respect to care to be confronted daily with the man he had wronged. Gradually Monty realized that "Nopper" was pursuing the most manly course open to him, and gave up the effort to dissuade him. He insisted upon leaving New York, as there was no opportunity to redeem himself in the metropolis.

"I've made up my mind, Monty, to go out west, up in the mountains perhaps. There's no telling, I may stumble on a gold mine up there—and—well, that seems to be the only chance I have to restore what I have taken from you."

"By Jove, Nopper, I have it!" cried Monty. "If you must go, I'll stake you in the hunt for gold."

In the end "Nopper" consented to follow Brewster's advice, and it was agreed that they

should share equally all that resulted from his
prospecting tour. Brewster "grub-staked"
him for a year, and before the end of the week
a new tenderfoot was on his way to the Rocky
Mountains.

CHAPTER XVIII

THE PRODIGAL AT SEA

Harrison's departure left Brewster in sore straits. It forced him to settle down to the actual management of his own affairs. He was not indolent, but this was not the kind of work he cared to encourage. The private accounts he had kept revealed some appalling facts when he went over them carefully one morning at four o'clock, after an all-night session with the ledger. With infinite pains he had managed to rise to something over $450,000 in six months. But to his original million it had been necessary to add $58,550 which he had realized from Lumber and Fuel and some of his other "unfortunate" operations. At least $40,000 would come to him ultimately through the sale of furniture and other belongings, and then there would be something like $20,000 interest to consider. But luck had aided him in getting rid of his money. The bank failure had cost him $113,468.25, and "Nopper" Harrison had helped him to the extent of $60,000. The reckless but deter-

mined effort to give a ball had cost $30,000.
What he had lost during his illness had been
pretty well offset by the unlucky concert tour.
The Florida trip, including medical attention,
the cottage and living expenses, had entailed
the expenditure of $18,500, and his princely
dinners and theater parties had footed up
$31,000. Taking all the facts into considera-
tion, he felt that he had done rather well as far
as he had gone, but the hardest part of the
undertaking was yet to come. He was still in
possession of an enormous sum which must
disappear before September 23d. About
$40,000 had already been expended in the
yachting project.

He determined to begin at once a systematic
campaign of extinction. It had been his intention before sailing to dispose of many household articles, either by sale or gift. As he did
not expect to return to New York before the
latter part of August, this would minimize the
struggles of the last month. But the prospective "profit" to be acquired from keeping his
apartment open was not to be overlooked. He
could easily count upon a generous sum for
salaries and running expenses. Once on the
other side of the Atlantic, he hoped that new
opportunities for extravagance would present

themselves, and he fancied he could leave
the final settlement of his affairs for the last
month.   As the day for sailing approached,
the world again seemed bright to this most
mercenary of spendthrifts.

A farewell consultation with his attorneys
proved encouraging, for to them his chances to
win the extraordinary contest seemed of the
best.   He was in high spirits as he left them,
exhilarated by the sensation that the world lay
before him.   In the elevator he encountered
Colonel Prentiss Drew.   On both sides the
meeting was not without its difficulties.   The
Colonel had been dazed by the inexplicable
situation between Monty and his daughter,
whose involutions he found hard to understand.
Her summary of the effort she had made to
effect a reconciliation, after hearing the story
of the bank, was rather vague.   She had done
her utmost, she said, to be nice to him and
make him feel that she appreciated his generosity, but he took it in the most disagreeable
fashion.   Colonel Drew knew that things were
somehow wrong; but he was too strongly an
American father to interfere in a matter of the
affections.   It distressed him, for he had a
liking for Monty, and Barbara's "society
judgments," as he called them, had no weight

with him.   When he found himself confronted
with Brewster in the elevator, the old warmth
revived and the old hope that the quarrel
might have an end.   His greeting was cheery.

"You have not forgotten, Brewster," he said,
as they shook hands, "that you have a dollar
or two with us?"

"No," said Monty, "not exactly.   And I
shall be calling upon you for some of it very
soon.   I'm off on Thursday for a cruise in the
Mediterranean."

"I've heard something of it."   They had
reached the main floor and Colonel Drew had
drawn his companion out of the crowd into the
rotunda.   "The money is at your disposal at
any moment   But aren't you setting a pretty
lively pace, my boy?   You know I've always
liked you, and I knew your grandfather rather
well.   He was a good old chap, Monty, and
he would hate to see you make ducks and
drakes of his fortune."

There was something in the Colonel's manner that softened Brewster, much as he hated
to take a reproof from Barbara's father.   Once
again he was tempted to tell the truth, but he
pulled himself up in time.   "It's a funny old
world, Colonel," he said; "and sometimes
one's nearest friend is a stranger.   I know I

seem a fool; but, after all, why isn't it good philosophy to make the most of a holiday and then settle back to work?"

"That is all very well, Monty," and Colonel Drew was entirely serious; "but the work is a hundred times harder after you have played to the limit. You'll find that you are way beyond it. It's no joke getting back into the harness."

"Perhaps you are right, Colonel, but at least I shall have something to look back upon— even if the worst comes." And Monty instinctively straightened his shoulders.

They turned to leave the building, and the Colonel had a moment of weakness.

"Do you know, Monty," he said, "my daughter is awfully cut up about this business. She is plucky and tries not to show it, but after all a girl doesn't get over that sort of thing all in a moment. I am not saying"—it seemed necessary to recede a step—"that it would be an easy matter to patch up. But I like you, Monty, and if any man could do it, you can."

"Colonel, I wish I might," and Brewster found that he did not hesitate. "For your sake I very much wish the situation were as simple as it seems. But there are some things a man can't forget, and—well—Barbara has shown in a dozen ways that she has no faith in me."

"Well, I've got faith in you, and a lot of it. Take care of yourself, and when you get back you can count on me.   Good-bye."

On Thursday morning the "Flitter" steamed off down the bay, and the flight of the prodigal grandson was on.   No swifter, cleaner, handsomer boat ever sailed out of the harbor of New York, and it was a merry crowd that she carried out to sea.   Brewster's guests numbered twenty-five, and they brought with them a liberal supply of maids, valets, and luggage. It was not until many weeks later that he read the vivid descriptions of the weighing of the anchor which were printed in the New York papers, but by that time he was impervious to their ridicule.

On deck, watching the rugged silhouette of the city disappear into the mists, were Dan DeMille and Mrs. Dan, Peggy Gray, "Rip" Van Winkle, Reginald Vanderpool, Joe Bragdon, Dr. Lotless and his sister Isabel, Mr. and Mrs. Valentine — the official chaperon — and their daughter Mary, "Subway" Smith, Paul Pettingill, and some others hardly less distinguished.   As Monty looked over the eager crowd, he recognized with a peculiar glow that here were represented his best and truest friendships. The loyalty of these companions had been tested, and he knew that they would stand by him through everything.

There was no little surprise when it was learned that Dan DeMille was really to sail. Many of the idle voyagers ventured the opinion that he would try to desert the boat in mid-ocean if he saw a chance to get back to his club on a west-bound steamer. But DeMille, big, indolent, and indifferent, smiled carelessly, and hoped he wouldn't bother anybody if he "stuck to the ship" until the end.

For a time the sea and the sky and the talk of the crowd were enough for the joy of living. But after a few peaceful days there was a lull, and it was then that Monty gained the nickname of Aladdin, which clung to him. From somewhere, from the hold or the rigging or from under the sea, he brought forth four darkies from the south who strummed guitars and sang ragtime melodies. More than once during the voyage they were useful.

"Peggy," said Brewster one day, when the sky was particularly clear and things were quiet on deck, "on the whole I prefer this to crossing the North River on a ferry. I rather like it, don't you?"

"It seems like a dream," she cried, her eyes bright, her hair blowing in the wind.

"And, Peggy, do you know what I tucked away in a chest down in my cabin? A lot of books that you like—some from the old garret. I've saved them to read on rainy days."

Peggy did not speak, but the blood began to creep into her face and she looked wistfully across the water. Then she smiled.

"I didn't know you could save anything," she said, weakly.

"Come now, Peggy, that is too much."

"I didn't mean to hurt you. But you must not forget, Monty, that there are other years to follow this one. Do you know what I mean?"

"Peggy, dear, please don't lecture me," he begged, so piteously that she could not be serious.

"The class is dismissed for to-day, Monty," she said, airily. "But the professor knows his duty and won't let you off so easily next time."

CHAPTER XIX

At Gibraltar, Monty was handed an ominous-looking cablegram which he opened tremblingly.

To MONTGOMERY BREWSTER,
> Private Yacht Flitter, Gibraltar.

There is an agitation to declare for free silver. You may have twice as much to spend. Hooray.

JONES.

To which Monty responded:

Defeat the measure at any cost. The more the merrier, and charge it to me.   BREWSTER.

P. S. Please send many cables and mark them collect.

The Riviera season was fast closing, and the possibilities suggested by Monte Carlo were too alluring to the host to admit of a long stop at Gibraltar. But the DeMilles had letters to one of the officers of the garrison, and Brewster could not overlook the opportunity to give an elaborate dinner. The success of the affair may best be judged by the fact that the "Flitter's" larder required an entirely new stock the next day. The officers and ladies of the garrison were asked, and Monty would have entertained the entire regiment with beer and sandwiches if his friends had not interfered.

"It might cement the Anglo-American alliance," argued Gardner, "but your pocket-book needs cementing a bit more."

Yet the pocket-book was very wide open, and Gardner's only consolation lay in a tall English girl whom he took out to dinner. For the others there were many compensations, as the affair was brilliant and the new element a pleasant relief from the inevitable monotony.

It was after the guests had gone ashore that Monty discovered Mr. and Mrs. Dan holding a tête-à-tête in the stern of the boat.

"I am sorry to break this up," he interrupted, "but as the only conscientious chaperon in the party, I must warn you that your behavior is already being talked about. The idea of a sedate old married couple sitting out here alone watching the moon! It's shocking."

"I yield to the host," said Dan, mockingly. "But I shall be consumed with jealousy until you restore her to me."

Monty noticed the look in Mrs. Dan's eyes as she watched her husband go, and marked a new note in her voice as she said, "How this trip is bringing him out."

"He has just discovered," Monty observed, "that the club is not the only place in the world."

"It's a funny thing," she answered, "that Dan should have been so misunderstood. Do you know that he relentlessly conceals his best side? Down underneath he is the kind of man who could do a fine thing very simply."

"My dear Mrs. Dan, you surprise me. It looks to me almost as though you had fallen in love with Dan yourself."

"Monty," she said, sharply, "you are as blind as the rest. Have you never seen that before? I have played many games, but I have always come back to Dan. Through them all I have known that he was the only thing possible to me—the only thing in the least desirable. It's a queer muddle that one should be tempted to play with fire even when one is monotonously happy. I've been singed once or twice. But Dan is a dear and he has always helped me out of a tight place. He knows. No one understands better than Dan. And perhaps if I were less wickedly human, he would not care for me so much."

Monty listened at first in a sort of daze, for he had unthinkingly accepted the general opinion of the DeMille situation. But there were tears in her eyes for a moment, and the tone of her voice was convincing. It came to him with unpleasant distinctness that he had been all kinds of a fool. Looking back over his intercourse with her, he realized that the situation had been clear enough all the time.

"How little we know our friends!" he exclaimed, with some bitterness. And a moment later, "I've liked you a great deal Mrs. Dan, for a long time, but to-night—well, to-night I am jealous of Dan."

The "Flitter" saw some rough weather in making the trip across the Bay of Lyons. She was heading for Nice when an incident occurred that created the first real excitement experienced on the voyage. A group of passengers in the main saloon was discussing, more or less stealthily, Monty's "misdemeanors," when Reggy Vanderpool sauntered lazily in, his face displaying the only sign of interest it had shown in days.

"Funny predicament I was just in," he drawled. "I want to ask what a fellow should have done under the circumstances."

"I'd have refused the girl," observed "Rip" Van Winkle, laconically.

"Girl had nothing to do with it, old chap," went on Reggy, dropping into a chair. "Fellow fell overboard a little while ago,'' he went on, calmly. There was a chorus of cries and Brewster was forgotten for a time. ''One of the sailors, you know. He was doing something in the rigging near where I was standing. Puff! off he went into the sea, and there he was puttering around in the water.''

''Oh, the poor fellow,'' cried Miss Valentine.

''I'd never set eyes on him before—perfect stranger. I wouldn't have hesitated a minute, but the deck was crowded with a lot of his friends. One chap was his bunkie. So, really now, it wasn't my place to jump in after him. He could swim a bit, and I yelled to him to hold up and I'd tell the captain. Confounded captain wasn't to be found though. Somebody said he was asleep. In the end I told the mate. By this time we were a mile away from the place where he went overboard, and I told the mate I didn't think we could find him if we went back. But he lowered some boats and they put back fast. Afterwards I got to thinking about the matter. Of course if I had known him—if he had been one of you—it would have been different.''

''And you were the best swimmer in college, you miserable rat,'' exploded Dr. Lotless.

There was a wild rush for the upper deck,

and Vanderpool was not the hero of the hour.
The "Flitter" had turned and was steaming
back over her course. Two small boats were
racing to the place where Reggy's unknown
had gone over.

"Where is Brewster?" shouted Joe Bragdon.

"I can't find him, sir," answered the first
mate.

"He ought to know of this," cried Mr. Valentine.

"There! By the eternal, they are picking
somebody up over yonder," exclaimed the
mate. "See! that first boat has laid to and
they are dragging—yes, sir, he's saved!"

A cheer went up on board and the men in
the small boats waved their caps in response.
Everybody rushed to the rail as the "Flitter"
drew up to the boats, and there was intense
excitement on board. A gasp of amazement
went up from every one.

Monty Brewster, drenched but smiling, sat
in one of the boats, and leaning limply against
him, his head on his chest, was the sailor who
had fallen overboard. Brewster had seen the
man in the water and, instead of wondering
what his antecedents were, leaped to his assistance. When the boat reached him his unconscious burden was a dead weight and his own

strength was almost gone.   Another minute or two and both would have gone to the bottom.

As they hauled Monty over the side he shivered for an instant, grasped the first little hand that sought his so frantically, and then turned to look upon the half-dead sailor.

"Find out that boy's name, Mr. Abertz, and see that he has the best of care.   Just before he fainted out there he murmured something about his mother.   He wasn't thinking of himself even then, you see.   And Bragdon"—this in a lower voice—"will you see that his wages are properly increased?   Hello, Peggy!   Look out, you'll get wet to the skin if you do that."

CHAPTER XX

If Montgomery Brewster had had any misgivings about his ability to dispose of the
balance of his fortune they were dispelled
very soon after his party landed in the Riviera.
On the pretext that the yacht required a
thorough "house cleaning" Brewster transferred his guests to the hotel of a fascinating
village which was near the sea and yet quite
out of the world. The place was nearly empty
at the time and the proprietor wept tears of
joy when Monty engaged for his party the
entire first floor of the house with balconies
overlooking the blue Mediterranean and a separate dining-room and salon. Extra servants
were summoned, and the Brewster livery was
soon a familiar sight about the village. The
protests of Peggy and the others were only
silenced when Monty threatened to rent a villa
and go to housekeeping.

The town quickly took on the appearance of
entertaining a royal visitor, and a number of
shops were kept open longer than usual in the

hope that their owners might catch some of the American's money. One morning Philippe, the hotel proprietor, was trying to impress Brewster with a gesticulatory description of the glories of the Bataille de Fleurs. It seemed quite impossible to express the extent of his regret that the party had not arrived in time to see it.

"This is quite another place at that time," he said ecstatically. "C'est magnifique! c'est superbe! If monsieur had only seen it!"

"Why not have another all to ourselves?" asked Monty. But the suggestion was not taken seriously.

Nevertheless the young American and his host were in secret session for the rest of the morning, and when the result was announced at luncheon there was general consternation. It appeared that ten days later occurred the fête day of some minor saint who had not for years been accorded the honor of a celebration. Monty proposed to revive the custom by arranging a second carnival.

"You might just as well not come to the Riviera at all," he explained, "if you can't see a carnival. It's a simple matter, really. I offer one prize for the best decorated carriage and another to the handsomest lady. Then everyone puts on a domino and a mask, throws confetti at everyone else, and there you are."

"I suppose you will have the confetti made of thousand franc notes, and offer a house and lot as a prize." And Bragdon feared that his sarcasm was almost insulting.

"Really, Monty, the scheme is ridiculous," said DeMille, "the police won't allow it."

"Won't they though!" said Monty, exultantly. "The chief happens to be Philippe's brother-in-law, and we had him on the telephone. He wouldn't listen to the scheme until we agreed to make him grand marshal of the parade. Then he promised the coöperation of the entire force and hoped to interest his colleague, the chief of the fire department."

"The parade will consist of two gendarmes and the Brewster party in carriages," laughed Mrs. Dan. "Do you expect us to go before or after the bakery carts?"

"We review the procession from the hotel," said Monty. "You needn't worry about the fête. It's going to be great. Why, an Irishman isn't fonder of marching than these people are of having a carnival."

The men in the party went into executive session as soon as Monty had gone to interview the local authorities, and seriously considered taking measures to subdue their host's eccentricities. But the humor of the scheme appealed to them too forcibly, and almost before they knew it they were making plans for the carnival.

"Of course we can't let him do it, but it would be sport," said "Subway" Smith. "Think of a cake-walk between gendarmes and blanchiseuses."

"I always feel devilish the moment I get a mask on," said Vanderpool, "and you know, by Jove, I haven't felt that way for years."

"That settles it, then," said DeMille. "Monty would call it off himself if he knew how it would affect Reggie."

Monty returned with the announcement that the mayor of the town would declare a holiday if the American could see his way to pay for the repairs on the mairie roof. A circus, which was traveling in the neighborhood, was guaranteed expenses if it would stop over and occupy the square in front of the Hôtel de Ville. Brewster's enthusiasm was such that no one could resist helping him, and for nearly a week his friends were occupied in superintending the erection of triumphal arches and encouraging the shopkeepers to do their best. Although the scheme had been conceived in

the spirit of a lark it was not so received by
the townspeople. They were quite serious in
the matter. The railroad officials sent adver-
tisements broadcast, and the local curé called
to thank Brewster for resurrecting, as it were,
the obscure saint. The expression of his gratitude was so mingled with flattery and appeal
that Monty could not overlook the hint that
a new altar piece had long been needed.

The great day finally arrived, and no carnival
could have been more bizarre or more successful. The morning was devoted to athletics and
the side shows. The pompiers won the tug of
war, and the people marveled when Monty
duplicated the feats of the strong man in the
circus. DeMille was called upon for a speech,
but knowing only ten words of French, he
graciously retired in favor of the mayor, and
that pompous little man made the most of a
rare opportunity. References to Franklin and
Lafayette were so frequent that "Subway"
Smith intimated that a rubber stamp must have
been used in writing the address.

The parade took place in the afternoon, and
proved quite the feature of the day. The question of precedence nearly overturned Monty's
plans, but the chief of police was finally made
to see that if he were to be chief marshal it

was only fair that the pompiers should march ahead of the gendarmes. The crew of the "Flitter" made a wonderful showing. It was led by the yacht's band, which fairly outdid Sousa in noise, though it was less unanimous in the matter of time. All the fiacres came at the end, but there were so many of them and the line of march was so short that at times they were really leading the procession despite the gallant efforts of the grand marshal.

From the balcony of the hotel Monty and his party pelted those below with flowers and confetti. More allusions to Franklin and Lafayette were made when the curé and the mayor halted the procession and presented Monty with an address richly engrossed on imitation parchment. Then the school children sang and the crowd dispersed to meet again in the evening.

At eight o'clock Brewster presided over a large banquet, and numbered among his guests everyone of distinction in the town. The wives were also invited and Franklin and Lafayette were again alluded to. Each of the men made at least one speech, but "Subway" Smith's third address was the hit of the evening. Knowing nothing but English he had previously clung consistently to that language, but the third and final address seemed to demand something more friendly and genial. With a sweeping bow and with all the dignity of a statesman he began:

"Mesdames et Messieurs: J'ai, tu as, il a, nous avons," — with a magnificent gesture, "vous avez." The French members of the company were not equal to his pronunciation and were under the impression that he was still talking English. They were profoundly impressed with his deference and grace and accorded his preamble a round of applause. The Americans did their utmost to persuade him to be seated, but their uproar was mistaken by the others for enthusiasm, and the applause grew louder than ever. "Subway" held up his hand for silence, and his manner suggested that he was about to utter some peculiarly important thought. He waited until a pin fall could have been heard before he went on.

"Maître corbeau sur un arbre perché—" he finished the speech as he was being carried bodily from the room by DeMille and Bragdon. The Frenchmen then imagined that Smith's remarks had been insulting, and his friends had silenced him on that account. A riot seemed imminent when Monty succeeded in restoring silence, and with a few tactful remarks about Franklin and Lafayette quieted the excited guests.

The evening ended with fireworks and a dance in the open air,—a dance that grew gay under the masks. The wheels had been well oiled and there was no visible failure of the carnival spirit. To Brewster it seemed a mad game, and he found it less easy to play a part behind the foolish mask than he expected. His own friends seemed to elude him, and the coquetries of the village damsels had merely a fleeting charm. He was standing apart to watch the glimmering crowd when he was startled by a smothered cry. Turning to investigate, he discovered a little red domino, unmistakably frightened, and trying to release herself from a too ardent Punchinello. Monty's arrival prevented him from tearing off the girl's mask and gave him an entirely new conception of the strenuous life. He arose fuming and sputtering, but he was taken in hand by the crowd and whirled from one to another in whimsical mockery. Meanwhile Monty, unconscious that his mask had dropped during the encounter, was astonished to feel the little hand of the red domino on his arm and to hear a voice not all unfamiliar in his ear.

"Monty, you are a dear. I love you for that. You looked like a Greek athlete. Do you know —it was foolish—but I really was frightened."

"Child, how could it have happened?" he whispered, leading her away. "Fancy my little Peggy with no one to look after her. What a beast I was to trust you to Pettingill. I might have known the chump would have been knocked out by all this color." He stopped to look down at her and a light came into his eyes. "Little Peggy in the great world," he smiled; "you are not fit. You need—well, you need—just me."

But Mrs. Valentine had seen him as he stood revealed, and came up in search of Peggy. It was almost morning, she told her, and quite time to go back to the hotel and sleep. So in Bragdon's charge they wandered off, a bit reluctantly, a bit lingeringly.

It was not until Monty was summoned to rescue "Reggie" Vanderpool from the stern arm of the law that he dicovered the identity of Punchinello. Manifestly he had not been in a condition to recognize his assailant, and a subsequent disagreement had driven the first out of his head. The poor boy was sadly bruised about the face and his arrest had probably saved him from worse punishment.

"I told you I couldn't wear a mask," he explained ruefully as Monty led him home. "But how could I know that he could hear me all the time?"

The day after the carnival Brewster drove his guests over to Monte Carlo. He meant to stay only long enough to try his luck at the tables and lose enough to make up for the days at sea when his purse was necessarily idle. Swearengen Jones was forgotten, and soon after his arrival he began to plunge. At first he lost heavily, and it was with difficulty that he concealed his joy. Peggy Gray was watching him, and in whispers implored him to stop, but Mrs. Dan excitedly urged him to continue until the luck changed. To the girl's chagrin it was the more reckless advice that he followed. In so desperate a situation he felt that he could not stop. But his luck turned too soon.

"I can't afford to give up," he said, miserably, to himself, after a time. "I'm already a winner by five thousand dollars, and I must at least get rid of that."

Brewster became the center of interest to those who were not playing and people marveled at his luck. They quite misinterpreted his eagerness and the flushed anxious look with

which he followed each spin of the wheel. He
had chosen a seat beside an English duchess
whose practice it was to appropriate the winnings of the more inexperienced players, and
he was aware that many of his gold pieces
were being deliberately stolen. Here he
thought was at least a helping hand, and he
was on the point of moving his stack toward
her side when DeMille interfered. He had
watched the duchess, and had called the
croupier's attention to her neat little method.
But that austere individual silenced him by
saying in surprise, "Mais c'est madame la
duchesse, que voulez-vous?"

Not to be downed so easily, DeMille
watched the play from behind Monty's chair
and cautioned his friend at the first opportunity.

"Better cash in and change your seat,
Monty. They're robbing you," he whispered.

"Cash in when I'm away ahead of the game?
Never!" and Monty did his best to assume
a joyful tone.

At first he played with no effort at system,
piling his money flat on the numbers which
seemed to have least chance of winning, but
he simply could not lose. Then he tried to
reverse different systems he had heard of, but

they turned out to be winners. Finally in desperation he began doubling on one color in the hope that he would surely lose in the end, but his particular fate was against him. With his entire stake on the red the ball continued to fall in the red holes until the croupier announced that the bank was broken.

Dan DeMille gathered in the money and counted forty thousand dollars before he handed it to Monty. His friends were over-joyed when he left the table, and wondered why he looked so downhearted. Inwardly he berated himself for not taking Peggy's advice.

"I'm so glad for your sake that you did not stop when I asked you, Monty, but your luck does not change my belief that gambling is next to stealing," Peggy was constrained to say as they went to supper.

"I wish I had taken your advice," he said gloomily.

"And missed the fortune you have won? How foolish of you, Monty! You were a loser by several thousand dollars then," she objected with whimsical inconsistency.

"But, Peggy," he said quietly, looking deep into her eyes, "it would have won me your respect."

CHAPTER XXI

Monty's situation was desperate. Only a little more than six thousand dollars had been spent on the carnival and no opportunity of annihilating the roulette winnings seemed to offer itself. His experience at Monte Carlo did not encourage him to try again, and Peggy's attitude toward the place was distinctly antagonistic. The Riviera presenting no new opportunities for extravagance, it became necessary to seek other worlds.

"I never before understood the real meaning of the phrase 'tight money,'" thought Monty. "Lord, if it would only loosen a bit and stay loosened." Something must be done, he realized, to earn his living. Perhaps the rôle of the princely profligate would be easier in Italy than anywhere else. He studied the outlook from every point of view, but there were moments when it seemed hopeless. Baedeker was provokingly barren of suggestions for extravagance and Monty grew impatient of the book's small economies. Noticing some chapters on the Italian lakes, in an inspired moment he remembered that Pettingill had once lost his heart to a villa on the Lake of Como. Instantly a new act of the comedy presented itself to him. He sought out Pettingill and demanded a description of his castle in the air.

"Oh, it's a wonder," exclaimed the artist, and his eyes grew dreamy. "It shines out at you with its white terraces and turrets like those fascinating castles that Maxfield Parrish draws for children. It is fairyland. You expect to wake and find it gone."

"Oh, drop that, Petty," said Brewster, "or it will make you poetical. What I want to know is who owns it and is it likely to be occupied at this season?"

"It belongs to a certain marquise, who is a widow with no children. They say she has a horror of the place for some reason and has never been near it. It is kept as though she were to turn up the next day, but except for the servants it is always deserted."

"The very thing," declared Brewster; "Petty, we'll have a house-party."

"You'd better not count on that, Monty. A man I know ran across the place once and tried for a year to buy it. But the lady has ideas of her own."

"Well, if you wish to give him a hint or two about how to do things, watch me. If you don't spend two weeks in your dream-castle, I will cut the crowd and sail for home." He secured the name of the owner, and found that Pettingill had even a remote idea of the address of her agent. Armed with these facts he set out in search of a courier, and through Philippe he secured a Frenchman named Bertier, who was guaranteed to be surprisingly ingenious in providing methods of spending money. To him Brewster confided his scheme, and Bertier realized with rising enthusiasm that at last he had secured a client after his own heart. He was able to complete the address of the agent of the mysterious marquise, and an inquiry was immediately telegraphed to him.

The agent's reply would have been discouraging to anyone but Brewster. It stated that the owner had no intention of leasing her forsaken castle for any period whatever. The profligate learned that a fair price for an estate of that kind for a month was ten thousand francs, and he wired an offer of five times that sum for two weeks. The agent replied that some delay would be necessary while he communicated with his principal.

Delay was the one word that Brewster did not understand, so he wired him an address in Genoa, and the "Flitter" was made ready for sea. Steam had been kept up, and her coal account would compare favorably with that of an ocean liner. Philippe was breathless with joy when he was paid in advance for another month at the hotel, on the assumption that the party might be moved to return at any moment. The little town was gay at parting and Brewster and his guests were given a royal farewell.

At Genoa the mail had accumulated and held the attention of the yacht to the exclusion of everything else. Brewster was somewhat crestfallen to learn that the lady of the villa haughtily refused his princely offer. He won the life-long devotion of his courier by promptly increasing it to one hundred thousand francs. When this too met with rejection, there was a pause and a serious consultation between the two.

"Bertier," exclaimed Brewster, "I must have the thing now. What's to be done? You've got to help me out."

But the courier, prodigal as he was of gestures, had no words which seemed pertinent.

"There must be some way of getting at this

marquise," Monty continued reflectively. "What are her tastes? Do you know anything about her?"

Suddenly the face of the courier grew bright. "I have it," he said, and then he faltered. "But the expense, monsieur—it would be heavy."

"Perhaps we can meet it," suggested Monty, quietly. "What's the idea?"

It was explained, with plenty of action to make it clear. The courier had heard in Florence that madame la marquise had a passion for automobiles. But with her inadequate fortune and the many demands upon it, it was a weakness not readily gratified. The machine she had used during the winter was by no means up-to-date. Possibly if monsieur— yet it was too much—no villa—

But Brewster's decision was made. "Wire the fellow," he said, "that I will add to my last offer a French machine of the latest model and the best make. Say, too, that I would like immediate possession."

He secured it, and the crowd was transferred at once to fairyland. There were protests, of course, but these Brewster had grown to expect and he was learning to carry things with a high hand. The travelers had been preceded

by Bertier, and the greeting they received
from the steward of the estate and his innumer-
able assistants was very Italian and full of
color. A break in their monotony was
welcome.

The loveliness of the villa and its grounds,
which sloped down to the gentle lake, silenced
criticism. For a time it was supremely satisfy-
ing to do nothing. Pettingill wandered about
as though he could not believe it was real.
He was lost in a kind of atmosphere of ecstasy.
To the others, who took it more calmly, it was
still a sort of paradise. Those who were
happy found in it an intensification of happiness, and to those who were sad it offered the
tenderest opportunities for melancholy. Mrs.
Dan told Brewster that only a poet could have
had this inspiration. And Peggy added,
"Anything after this would be an anti-climax.
Really, Monty, you would better take us home."

"I feel like the boy who was shut in a closet
for punishment and found it the place where
they kept the jam," said "Subway." "It is
almost as good as owning Central Park."

The stables were well equipped and the
days wore on in a wonderful peace. It was on
a radiant afternoon, when twelve of the crowd
had started out, after tea, for a long ride toward

Lugano, that Monty determined to call Peggy
Gray to account. He was certain that she had
deliberately avoided him for days and weeks,
and he could find no reason for it. Hour after
hour he had lain awake wondering where he
had failed her, but the conclusion of one
moment was rejected the next. The Monte
Carlo episode seemed the most plausible cause,
yet even before that he had noticed that whenever he approached her she managed to be
talking with some one else. Two or three
times he was sure she had seen his intention
before she took refuge with Mrs. Dan or Mary
Valentine or Pettingill. The thought of the
last name gave Monty a sudden thrill. What
if it were he who had come between them? It
troubled him, but there were moments when
the idea seemed impossible. As they mounted
and started off, the exhilaration of the ride
made him hopeful. They were to have dinner
in the open air in the shadow of an abbey ruin
some miles away, and the servants had been
sent ahead to prepare it. It went well, and
with Mrs. Dan's help the dinner was made
gay. On the return Monty who was off last
spurred up his horse to join Peggy. She
seemed eager to be with the rest and he lost
no time with a preamble.

"Do you know, Peggy," he began, "something seems to be wrong, and I am wondering what it is."

"Why, what do you mean, Monty?" as he paused.

"Every time I come near you, child, you seem to have something else to do. If I join the group you are in, it is the signal for you to break away."

"Nonsense, Monty, why should I avoid you? We have known one another much too long for that." But he thought he detected some contradiction in her eyes, and he was right. The girl was afraid of him, afraid of the sensations he awoke, afraid desperately of betrayal.

"Pettingill may appeal to you," he said, and his voice was serious, "but you might at least be courteous to me."

"How absurd you are, Monty Brewster." The girl grew hot. "You needn't think that your million gives you the privilege of dictating to all of your guests."

"Peggy, how can you," he interjected.

She went on ruthlessly. "If my conduct interferes with your highness's pleasure I can easily join the Prestons in Paris."

Suddenly Brewster remembered that Pettingill had spoken of the Prestons and expressed

a fleeting wish that he might be with them in
the Latin Quarter. "With Pettingill to follow,
I suppose," he said icily. "It would certainly
give you more privacy."

"And Mrs. Dan more opportunities," she
retorted as he dropped back toward the others.

The artist instantly took his place. The
next moment he had challenged her to a race
and they were flying down the road in the
moonlight. Brewster, not to be outdone, was
after them, but it was only a moment before
his horse shied violently at something black
in the road. Then he saw Peggy's horse gallop-
ing riderless. Instantly, with fear at his throat,
he had dismounted and was at the girl's side.
She was not hurt, they found, only bruised and
dazed and somewhat lamed. A girth had
broken and her saddle turned. The crowd
waited, silent and somewhat awed, until the
carriage with the servants came up and she
was put into it. Mrs. Dan's maid was there
and Peggy insisted that she would have no one
else. But as Monty helped her in, he had
whispered, "You won't go, child, will you?
How could things go on here?"

CHAPTER XXII

The peacefulness of fairyland was something which Brewster could not afford to continue, and with Bertier he was soon planning to invade it. The automobile which he was obliged to order for the mysterious marquise put other ideas into his head. It seemed at once absolutely necessary to give a coaching party in Italy, and as coaches of the right kind were hard to find there, and changes of horses most uncertain, nothing could be more simple and natural than to import automobiles from Paris. Looking into the matter, he found that they would have to be purchased outright, as the renting of five machines would put his credit to too severe a test. Accordingly Bertier telegraphed a wholesale order, which taxed the resources of the manufacturers and caused much complaint from some customers whose work was unaccountably delayed. The arrangement made by the courier was that they were to be taken back at a greatly reduced price at the end of six weeks. The machines were shipped at once, five to Milan, and one to the address of the mysterious marquise in Florence.

It was with a sharp regret that Monty broke into the idyl of the villa, for the witchery of the place had got into his blood. But a stern sense of duty, combined with the fact that the Paris chauffeurs and machines were due in Milan on Monday, made him ruthless. He was astonished that his orders to decamp were so meekly obeyed, forgetting that his solicitous guests did not know that worse extravagance lay beyond. He took them to Milan by train and lodged them with some splendor at the Hôtel Cavour. Here he found that the fame of the princely profligate had preceded him, and his portly host was all deference and attention. All regret, too, for monsieur was just too late to hear the wonderful company of artists who had been singing at La Scala. The season was but just ended. Here was an opportunity missed indeed, and Brewster's vexation brought out an ironical comment to Bertier. It rankled, but it had its effect. The courier proved equal to the emergency. Discovering that the manager of the company and the principal artists were still in Milan, he suggested to Brewster that a special performance would be very difficult to secure but might still be possible. His chief caught at the idea and authorized him to make every arrangement, reserving the entire house for his own party.

"But the place will look bare," protested the courier, aghast.

"Fill it with flowers, cover it with tapestries," commanded Brewster. "I put the affair in your hands, and I trust you to carry it through in the right way. Show them how it ought to be done."

Bertier's heart swelled within him at the thought of so glorious an opportunity. His fame, he felt, was already established in Italy. It became a matter of pride to do the thing handsomely, and the necessary business arrangements called out all his unused resources of delicacy and diplomacy. When it came to the decoration of the opera house, he called upon Pettingill for assistance, and together they superintended an arrangement which curtained off a large part of the place and reduced it to livable proportions. With the flowers and the lights, the tapestries and the great faded flags, it became something quite different from the usual empty theater.

To the consternation of the Italians, the work had been rushed, and it was on the even-

ing after their arrival in Milan that Brewster
conducted his friends in state to the Scala. It
was almost a triumphal progress, for he had
generously if unwittingly given the town the
most princely sensation in years, and curiosity
was abundant. Mrs. Valentine, who was in
the carriage with Monty, wondered openly why
they were attracting so much attention.

"They take us for American dukes and
princesses," explained Monty. "They never
saw a white man before."

"Perhaps they expected us to ride on buf-
faloes," said Mrs. Dan, "with Indian captives
in our train."

"No," "Subway" Smith protested, "I seem
to see disappointment in their faces. They
are looking for crowns and scepters and a
shower of gold coin. Really, Monty, you
don't play the game as you should. Why, I
could give you points on the potentate act
myself. A milk-white steed, a few clattering
attendants in gorgeous uniforms, a lofty nod
here and there, and little me distributing silver
in the rear."

"I wonder," exclaimed Mrs. Dan, "if they
don't get tired now and then of being poten-
tates. Can't you fancy living in palaces and
longing for a thatched cottage?"

"Easily," answered "Subway," with a laugh. "Haven't we tried it ourselves? Two months of living upon nothing but fatted calves is more than I can stand. We shall be ready for a home for dyspeptics if you can't slow down a bit, Monty."

Whereupon Mrs. Dan evolved a plan, and promptly began to carry it out by inviting the crowd to dinner the next night. Monty protested that they would be leaving Milan in the afternoon, and that this was distinctly his affair and he was selfish.

But Mrs. Dan was very sure. "My dear boy, you can't have things your own way every minute. In another month you will be quite spoiled. Anything to prevent that. My duty is plain. Even if I have to use heroic measures, you dine with me to-morrow."

Monty recognized defeat when he met it, and graciously accepted her very kind invitation. The next moment they drew up at the opera house and were ushered in with a deference only accorded to wealth. The splendor of the effect was overpowering to Brewster as well as to his bewildered guests. Aladdin, it seemed, had fairly outdone himself. The wonder of it was so complete that it was some time before they could settle down to the opera, which was Aida, given with an enthusiasm that only Italians can compass.

During the last intermission Brewster and Peggy were walking in the foyer. They had rarely spoken since the day of the ride but Monty noticed with happiness that she had on several occasions avoided Pettingill.

"I thought we had given up fairyland when we left the lakes, but I believe you carry it with you," she said.

"The trouble with this," Monty replied, "is that there are too many people about. My fairyland is to be just a little different."

"Your fairyland, Monty, will be built of gold and paved with silver You will sit all day cutting coupons in an office of alabaster."

"Peggy, do you too think me vulgar? It's a beastly parade, I know, but it can't stop now. You don't realize the momentum of the thing."

"You do it up to the handle," she put in. "And you are much too generous to be vulgar. But it worries me, Monty, it worries me desperately. It's the future I'm thinking of— your future, which is being swallowed up. This kind of thing can't go on. And what is to follow it? You are wasting your substance, and you are not making any life for yourself that opens out."

"Peggy," he answered very seriously, "you have got to trust me. I can't back out, but I'll tell you this. You shall not be disappointed in me in the end."

There was a mist before the girl's eyes as she looked at him. "I believe you, Monty," she said simply; "I shall not forget."

The curtain rose upon the next act, and something in the opera toward the end seemed to bring the two very close together. As they were leaving the theater, there was a note of regret from Peggy. "It has been perfect," she breathed, "yet, Monty, isn't it a waste that no one else should have seen it? Think of these poverty-stricken peasants who adore music and have never heard an opera."

"Well, they shall hear one now." Monty rose to it, but he felt like a hypocrite in concealing his chief motive. "We'll repeat the performance to-morrow night and fill the house with them."

He was as good as his word. Bertier was given a task the next day which was not to his taste. But with the assistance of the city authorities he carried it through. To them it was an evidence of insanity, but there was something princely about it and they were tolerant. The manager of the opera house was less complacent, and he had an exclamatory terror of the damage to his upholstery. But Brewster had discovered that in Italy gold is a panacea for all ills, and his prescriptions were liberal. To him the day was short, for Peggy's interest in the penance, as it came to be called, was so keen that she insisted on having a hand in the preliminaries. There was something about the partnership that appealed to Monty.

To her regret the DeMille dinner interfered with the opening of the performance, but Monty consoled her with the promise that the opera and its democratic audience should follow. During the day Mrs. Dan had been deep in preparations for her banquet, but her plans were elaborately concealed. They culminated at eight o'clock in the Cova not far from the Scala, and the dinner was eaten in the garden to the sound of music. Yet it was an effect of simplicity with which Mrs. Dan surprised her guests. They were prepared for anything but that, and when they were served with consommé, spaghetti—a concession to the chef—and chops and peas, followed by a salad and coffee, the gratitude of the crowd was quite beyond expression. In a burst of enthusiasm "Subway" Smith suggested a testimonial.

Monty complained bitterly that he himself had never received a ghost of a testimonial. He protested that it was not deserved.

"Why should you expect it?" exclaimed Pettingill, "when have you risen from terrapin and artichokes to chops and chicory? When have you given us nectar and ambrosia like this?"

Monty was defeated by a unanimous vote and Mrs. Dan's testimonial was assured. This matter settled, Peggy and Mrs. Valentine, with Brewster and Pettingill, walked over to the Scala and heard again the last two acts of Aida. But the audience was different, and the applause.

The next day at noon the chauffeurs from Paris reported for duty, and five gleaming French devil-wagons steamed off through the crowd in the direction of Venice. Through Brescia and Verona and Vicenza they passed, scattering largess of silver in their wake and leaving a trail of breathless wonder. Brewster found the pace too fast and by the time they reached Venice he had a wistful longing to take this radiant country more slowly. "But this is purely a business trip," he thought, "and I can't expect to enjoy it. Some day I'll come back and do it differently. I could spend hours in a gondola if the blamed things were not more expensive by the trip."

It was there that he was suddenly recalled to his duty from dreams of moonlight on the water, by a cablegram which demanded $324.00 before it could be read. It contained word for word the parable of the ten talents and ended with the simple word "Jones."

CHAPTER XXIII

AN OFFER OF MARRIAGE

The summer is scarcely a good time to visit Egypt, but Monty and his guests had a desire to see even a little of the northern coast of Africa. It was decided, therefore, that after Athens, the "Flitter," should go south. The yacht had met them at Naples after the automobile procession—a kind of triumphal progress,—was disbanded in Florence, and they had taken a hurried survey of Rome. By the middle of July the party was leaving the heat of Egypt and finding it not half bad. New York was not more than a month away as Brewster reckoned time and distance, and there was still too much money in the treasury. As September drew nearer he got into the habit of frequently forgetting Swearengen Jones until it was too late to retrace his steps. He was coming to the "death struggle," as he termed it, and there was something rather terrorizing in the fear that "the million might die hard." And so these last days and nights were glorious ones,

if one could have looked at them with unbiased, untroubled eyes. But every member of
his party was praying for the day when the
"Flitter" would be well into the broad Atlantic
and the worst over. At Alexandria Brewster
had letters to some Englishmen, and in the few
entertainments that he gave succeeded once
again, in fairly outdoing Aladdin.

A sheik from the interior was a guest at one
of Monty's entertainments. He was a burly,
hot-blooded fellow, with a densely-populated
harem, and he had been invited more as a
curiosity than as one to be honored. As he
came aboard the "Flitter," Monty believed
the invitation was more than justified. Mohammed was superb, and the women of the
party made so much of him that it was small
wonder that his head was turned. He fell
desperately in love with Peggy Gray on sight,
and with all the composure of a potentate who
has never been crossed he sent for Brewster
the next day and told him to "send her
around" and he would marry her. Monty's
blood boiled furiously for a minute or two, but
he was quick to see the wisdom of treating the
proposition diplomatically. He tried to make
it plain to the sheik that Miss Gray could not
accept the honor he wished to confer upon

her, but it was not Mohammed's custom to be
denied anything he asked for—especially anything feminine. He complacently announced
that he would come aboard that afternoon and
talk it over with Peggy.

Brewster looked the swarthy gentleman
over with unconcealed disgust in his eyes.
The mere thought of this ugly brute so much
as touching the hand of little Peggy Gray filled
him with horror, and yet there was something
laughable in the situation. He could not hide
the smile that came with the mind picture of
Peggy listening to the avowal of the sheik.
The Arab misinterpreted this exhibition of
mirth. To him the grin indicated friendship
and encouragement. He wanted to give
Brewster a ring as a pledge of affection, but
the American declined the offering and also
refused to carry a bag of jewels to Peggy.

"I'll let the old boy come aboard just to see
Peggy look a hole through him," he resolved.
"No matter how obnoxious it may be, it isn't
every girl who can say an oriental potentate
has asked her to marry him. If this camel-
herder gets disagreeable we. may tumble him
into the sea for a change."

With the best grace possible he invited the
sheik to come aboard and consult Miss Gray

in person. Mohammed was a good bit puzzled over the intimation that it would be necessary for him to plead for anything he had expressed a desire to possess. Brewster confided the news to "Rip" Van Winkle and "Subway" Smith, who had gone ashore with him, and the trio agreed that it would be good sport to let the royal proposal come as a surprise to Peggy. Van Winkle returned to the yacht at once, but his companions stayed ashore to do some shopping. When they approached the "Flitter" later on they observed an unusual commotion on deck.

Mohammed had not tarried long after their departure. He gathered his train together, selected a few costly presents that had been returned from the harem and advanced on the boat without delay. The captain of the "Flitter" stared long and hard at the gaily bedecked launches and then called to his first officer. Together they watched the ceremonious approach. A couple of brown-faced heralds came aboard first and announced the approach of the mighty chief. Captain Perry went forward to greet the sheik as he came over the side of the ship, but he was brushed aside by the advance guards. Half a hundred swarthy fellows crowded aboard and then came the sheik, the personification of pomp and pride.

"Where is she?" he asked in his native tongue. The passengers were by this time aware of the visitation, and began to straggle on deck, filled with curiosity.

"What the devil do you mean by coming aboard in this manner?" demanded the now irate Captain Perry, shoving a couple of retainers out of his path and facing the beaming suitor. An interpreter took a hand at this juncture and the doughty captain finally was made to understand the object of the visit. He laughed in the sheik's face and told the mate to call up a few jackies to drive the "dagoes" off. "Rip" Van Winkle interfered and peace was restored. The cruise had changed "Rip" into a happier and far more radiant creature, so it was only natural that he should have shared the secret with Mary Valentine. He had told the story of the sheik's demand to her as soon as he came aboard, and she had divulged it to Peggy the instant "Rip" was out of sight.

Brewster found the sheik sitting in state on the upper deck impatiently awaiting the appearance of his charmer. He did not know her name, but he had tranquilly commanded "Rip" to produce all of the women on board so that he might select Peggy from among them. Van Winkle and Bragdon, who now was in the secret, were preparing to march the ladies past the ruler when Monty came up.

"Has he seen Peggy?" he asked of Van Winkle.

"Not yet. She is dressing for the occasion."

"Well, wait and see what happens to him when she gets over the first shock," laughed Monty.

Just then the sheik discovered Peggy, who, pretty as a picture, drew near the strange group. To her amazement two slaves rushed forward and obstructed her passage long enough to beat their heads on the deck a few times, after which they arose and tendered two magnificent necklaces. She was prepared for the proposal, but this action disconcerted her; she gasped and looked about in perplexity. Her friends were smiling broadly and the sheik had placed his hands over his palpitating heart.

"Lothario has a pain," whispered "Rip" Van Winkle sympathetically, and Brewster laughed. Peggy did rot hesitate an instant after hearing the laugh. She walked straight toward the sheik. Her cheeks were pink and her eyes were flashing dangerously. The persistent brown slaves followed with the jewels, but she ignored them completely. Brave as she intended to be, she could not repress the shudder of repulsion that went over her as she looked full upon this eager Arab.

Graceful and slender she stood before the the burly Mohammed, but his ardor was not cooled by the presence of so many witnesses. With a thud he dropped to his knees, wabbling for a moment in the successful effort to maintain a poetic equilibrium. Then he began pouring forth volumes of shattered French, English and Arabic sentiment, accompanied by facial contortions so intense that they were little less than gruesome.

"Oh, joy of the sun supreme, jewel of the only eye, harken to the entreaty of Mohammed." It was more as if he were commanding his troops in battle than pleading for the tender compassion of a lady love. "I am come for you, queen of the sea and earth and sky. My boats are here, my camels there, and Mohammed promises you a palace in the sun-lit hills if you will but let him bask forever in the glory of your smile." All this was uttered in a mixture of tongues so atrocious that "Subway" Smith afterward described it as a salad. The retinue bowed impressively and two or three graceless Americans applauded as vigorously as if they were approving the actions of a well-drilled comic opera chorus. Sailors were hanging in the rigging, on the davits and over the deck house roof.

"Smile for the gentleman, Peggy," commanded Brewster delightedly. "He wants to take a short bask."

"You are very rude, Mr. Brewster," said Peggy turning upon him coldly. Then to the waiting, expectant sheik: "What is the meaning of this eloquence?"

Mohammed looked bewildered for a moment and then turned to the interpreter, who cleared up the mystery surrounding her English. For the next three or four minutes the air was filled with the "Jewels of Africa," "Star," "Sunlight," "Queen," "Heavenly Joy," "Pearl of the Desert," and other things in bad English, worse French, and perfect Arabic. He was making promises that could not be redeemed if he lived a thousand years. In conclusion the gallant sheik drew a long breath, screwed his face into a simpering grin and played his trump card in unmistakable English. It sounded pathetically like "You're a peach."

An indecorous roar went up from the white spectators and a jacky in the rigging, suddenly thinking of home, piped up with a bar or two from "The Star Spangled Banner."

Having accomplished what he considered to be his part of the ceremony the sheik arose and started toward his launch, coolly motioning for her to follow. So far as he was concerned the matter was closed. But Peggy, her heart thumping like a trip-hammer, her eyes full of excitement, implored him to stop for a moment.

"I appreciate this great honor, but I have a request to make," she said clearly. Mohammed paused irresolutely and in some irritation.

"Here's where the heathen gets it among the beads," whispered Monty to Mrs. Dan, and he called out: "Captain Perry, detail half a dozen men to pick up the beads that are about to slip from his majesty's neck."

CHAPTER XXIV

THE SHEIK'S STRATEGY

Peggy gave the sheik an entrancing smile, followed by a brief glance at the beaming Miss Valentine, who nodded her head approvingly.

"Won't you give me time to go below and pack my belongings that they may be sent ashore?" she asked naively.

"Thunder!" gasped Monty. "That's no way to turn him down."

"What do you mean, Monty Brewster?" she cried, turning upon him with flashing eyes.

"Why, you're encouraging the old guy," he protested, disappointment in every inflection.

"And what if I am? Isn't it my affair? I think I am right in suspecting that he has asked me to be his wife. Isn't it my privilege to accept him if I wish?"

Brewster's face was a study. He could not believe that she was in earnest, but there was a ghastly feeling that the joke was being turned on him. The rest of the company stared hard at the flushed Peggy and breathlessly awaited developments.

"It won't do to trifle with this chap, Peggy," said Monty, coming quite close to her. "Don't lead him on. He might get nasty if he thinks you're making sport of him."

"You are quite absurd, Monty," she cried, petulantly. "I am not making sport of him."

"Well, then, why don't you tell him to go about his business?"

"I don't see any beads lying around loose," said "Rip" tormentingly. The sheik impatiently said something to the interpreter and that worthy repeated it for Peggy's benefit.

"The Son of the Prophet desires that you be as quick as possible, Queen of the World. He tires of waiting and commands you to come with him at once."

Peggy winced and her eyes shot a brief look of scorn at the scowling sheik. In an instant, however, she was smiling agreeably and was turning toward the steps.

"Holy mackerel! Where are you going, Peggy?" cried Lotless, the first to turn fearful.

"To throw some things into my trunk," she responded airily. "Will you come with me, Mary?"

"Peggy!" cried Brewster angrily. "This has gone far enough."

"You should have spoken sooner, Monty," she said quietly.

"What are you going to do, Margaret?" cried Mrs. Dan," her eyes wide with amazement.

"I am going to marry the Son of the Prophet," she replied so decidedly that everyone gasped. A moment later she was surrounded by a group of excited women, and Captain Perry was calling the "jackies" forward in a voice of thunder.

Brewster pushed his way to her side, his face as white as death.

"This isn't a joke, Peggy," he cried. "Go below and I'll get rid of the sheik."

Just then the burly Algerian asserted himself. He did not like the way in which his adored one was being handled by the "white dogs," and with two spearmen he rushed up to Brewster, jabbering angrily.

"Stand back, you idiot, or I'll punch your head off," said Brewster, with sudden emphasis.

It was not until this moment that Peggy realized that there might be a serious side to the little farce she and Mary had decided to play for the punishment of Brewster. Terror suddenly took the place of mirth, and she clung frantically to Monty's arm.

"I was joking, Monty, only joking," she cried. "Oh, what have I done?"

"It's my fault," he exclaimed, "but I'll take care of you, never fear."

"Stand aside!" roared the sheik threateningly.

The situation was ominous. Frightened as they were the women could not flee, but stood as if petrified. Sailors eagerly swarmed to the deck.

"Get off this boat," said Monty, ominously calm, to the interpreter, "or we'll pitch you and your whole mob into the sea."

"Keep cool! Keep cool!" cried "Subway" Smith quickly. He stepped between Brewster and the angry suitor, and that action alone prevented serious trouble. While he parleyed with the sheik Mrs. DeMille hurried Peggy to a safe place below deck, and they were followed by a flock of shivering women. Poor Peggy was almost in tears and the piteous glances she threw at Brewster when he stepped between her and the impetuous sheik, who had started to follow, struck deep into his heart and made him ready to fight to the death for her.

It took nearly an hour to convince the Algerian that Peggy had misunderstood him and that American women were not to be wooed after the African fashion. He finally departed with his entire train, thoroughly dissatisfied and in high dudgeon. At first he threatened to take her by force; then he agreed to give her another day in which to make up her mind to go with him peaceably, and again he concluded that a bird in the hand was worth two in the bush.

Brewster stood gloomily on the outside of the excited group glowering upon the ugly suitor. Cooler heads had relegated him to this place of security during the diplomatic contest. The sheik's threats of vengeance were direful. He swore by somebody's beard that he would bring ten thousand men to establish his claim by force. His intense desire to fight for her then and there was quelled by Captain Perry's detachment of six lusty sailors, whose big bare fists were shaken vigorously under a few startled noses. It took all the fight out of the sheik and his train. Three retainers fell into the sea while trying to retreat as far as possible from danger.

Mohammed departed with the irate declaration that he would come another day and that the whole world would tremble at his approach. Disgusted with himself and afraid to meet the eyes of the other men, Brewster went below in search of Peggy. He took time to comfort the anxious women who crowded about him and then asked for Miss Gray. She was in her stateroom and would not come forth. When he knocked at the door a dismal, troubled voice from within told him to go away.

"Come out, Peggy; it's all over," he called.

"Please go away, Monty," she said.

"What are you doing in there?" There was a long pause, and then came the pitiful little wail: "I am unpacking, please, sir."

That night Brewster entertained on board the yacht, several resident French and English acquaintances being the guests of honor. The story of the day was told by Mrs. Dan DeMille, commissioned especially for the duty. She painted the scene so vividly that the guests laughed with joy over the discomfiture of the shiek. Peggy and Brewster found themselves looking sheepishly at one another now and then in the course of the recital. She purposely had avoided him during the evening, but she had gamely endured the raillery that came from the rest of the party. If she was a bit pale it was not surprising. Now that it was over the whole affair appalled her more than she could have suspected. When several of the guests of the evening soberly announced that Mohammed

was a dangerous man and even an object of
worry to the government she felt a strange catch
in her throat and her now mirthless eyes turned
instinctively to Brewster, who, it seemed, was
the sheik's special object of aversion.

The next day she and Monty talked it over.
The penitence of both was beautiful to behold.
Each denied the other the privilege of assuming all the blame and both were so happy that
Mohammed was little more than a preposition
in their conversation so far as prominence was
concerned. But all day long the harbor was
full of fisher boats, and at nightfall they still
were lolling about, sinister, restless, mysterious like purposeless buzzards. And the dark
men on board were taking up no fish, neither
were they minding the nets that lay dry and
folded in the bottom of their boats.

Far into the night there was revelry on board
the "Flitter," more guests having come out
from the city. The dark hours before the
dawn of day had arrived before they put off
for shore, but the fisher boats still were bob-
bing about in the black waters of the harbor.
The lights gradually disappeared from the
port-holes of the yacht, and the tired watch was
about to be relieved. Monty Brewster and Peggy
remained on deck after the guests had gone

over the side of the vessel. They were leaning over the rail aft listening to the jovial voices of the visitors as they grew fainter and fainter in the distance. The lights of the town were few, but they could plainly be seen from the offing.

"Are you tired, Peggy?" asked Brewster, with a touch of tenderness. Somehow of late he had often felt a strange desire to take her in his arms, and now it was strong upon him. She was very near, and there was a drooping weariness in her attitude which seemed to demand protection.

"I have a queer feeling that something awful is going to happen to-night, Monty," she answered, trouble in her soft voice.

"You're nervous, that's all," he said, "and you should get to sleep. Good-night." Their hands touched in the darkness, and the thrill that went over him told a truth of which he had been only vaguely conscious. The power of it made him exultant. Yet when he thought of her and her too quiet affection for him it left him despondent.

Something bumped against the side of the ship and a grating sound followed. Then came other gentle thuds combined with the soft swish of water disturbed. Peggy and Brewster were on the point of going below when their attention was caught by these strange sounds.

"What is it?" she asked as they paused irresolutely. He strode to the rail, the girl following close behind. Three sharp little whistles came from above and behind them, but before they had time even to speculate as to their meaning the result was in evidence.

Over the sides of the ship came shadowy forms as if by magic; at their backs panther-like bodies dropped to the deck with stealthy thuds, as if coming from the inky sky above. There was an instant of dreadful calm and then the crisis. A dozen sinewy forms hurled themselves upon Brewster, who, taken completely by surprise, was thrown to the deck in an instant, his attempt to cry out for help being checked by heavy hands. Peggy's scream was cut off as quickly, and paralyzed by terror, she felt herself engulfed in strong arms and smothered into silence. It all happened so quickly that there was no chance to give the alarm, no opportunity to resist.

Brewster felt himself lifted bodily, and then there was the sensation of falling. He struck something forcibly with all his weight and fell back with a crash to the deck. Afterward he found that the effort to throw him overboard had failed only because his assailants in their haste had hurled him against an unseen stanchion.   Peggy was borne forward and lowered swiftly into arms that deposited her roughly upon something hard.   There was a jerky, rocking motion, the sudden splash of oars, and then she knew no more.

The invaders had planned with a craftiness and patience that deserved success.   For hours they had waited, silently, watchfully, and with deadly assurance.   How they crept up to the "Flitter" in such numbers and how the more daring came aboard long before the blow was struck, no one ever explained.   So quickly and so accurately was the abduction performed that the boats were well clear of the yacht before alarm was given by one of the watch who had been overlooked in the careful assault.

Sleepy sailors rushed on deck with a promptness that was amazing.   Very quickly they had found and unbound Brewster, carried a couple of wounded shipmates below and had Captain Perry in his pajamas on deck to take command.

"The searchlight!" cried Brewster frantically. "The devils have stolen Miss Gray."

While swift hands were lowering the boats for the chase others were carrying firearms on deck.   The searchlight threw its mighty white

arm out over the water before many seconds
had passed, and eager eyes were looking for
the boats of the pillagers. The Arabs had
reckoned without the searchlight. Their fierce
exultation died suddenly when the mysterious
streak of light shot into the sky and then swept
down upon the sea, hunting them out of the
darkness like a great and relentless eye.

The "Flitter's" boats were in the water and
manned by sturdy oarsmen before the glad cry
went up that the robber fleet had been discovered. They were so near the yacht that it
was evident the dusky tribesmen were poor
oarsmen. In the clear light from the ship's
deck they could be seen paddling wildly, their
white robes fluttering as though inspired by
fear. There were four boats, all of them
crowded to the gunwales.

"Keep the light on them, captain," shouted
Monty from below. "Try to pick out the
boat that has Miss Gray on board. Pull away,
boys! This means a hundred dollars to every
one of you—yes, a thousand if we have to fight
for her!"

"Kill every damned one of them, Mr. Brewster," roared the captain, who had retired
behind a boat when he became aware of the
presence of women on deck.

Three boats shot away from the side of the yacht, Brewster and Joe Bragdon in the first, both armed with rifles.

"Let's take a shot at 'em," cried a sailor who stood in the stern with his finger on a trigger.

"Don't do that! We don't know what boat holds Peggy," commanded Brewster. "Keep cool, boys, and be ready to scrap if we have to." He was half mad with fear and anxiety, and he was determined to exterminate the bands of robbers if harm came to the girl in their power.

"She's in the second boat," came the cry from the yacht, and the searchlight was kept on that particular object almost to the exclusion of the others. But Captain Perry saw the wisdom of keeping all of them clearly located in order to prevent trickery.

Brewster's brawny sailor boys came up like greyhounds, cheering as they dashed among the boats of the fugitives. Three or four shots were fired into the air by the zealous American lads, and there were loud cries from the Arabs as they veered off panic-stricken. Monty's boat was now in the path of light and not far behind the one which held Peggy. He was standing in the bow.

"Take care of the others!" he called back to his followers. "We'll go after the leaders."

The response from behind was a cheer, a half dozen shots and some of the most joyous profanity that ever fell from the lips of American sailors, mingled with shrieks from the boats they were to"take care of."

"Stop!" Brewster shouted to the Arabs. "Stop, or we'll kill every one of you!" His boat was not more than fifty feet from the other.

Suddenly a tall, white-robed figure arose in the middle of the Egyptian craft, and a moment later the pursuers saw Peggy's form passed up to him. She was instantly clasped by one of nis long arms, and the other was lifted high above her. A gleaming knife was held in the upraised hand.

"Fire on us if you dare!" came in French from the tall Arab. "Dog of an American, she shall die if you come near her!"

CHAPTER XXV

THE RESCUE OF PEGGY

Brewster's heart almost ceased beating, and every vestige of color left his face. Clear and distinct in the light from the yacht the Arab and his burden were outlined against the black screen beyond. There was no mistaking the earnestness of the threat, nor could the witnesses doubt the ghastly intention of the long, cruel knife that gleamed on high. Peggy's body served as a shield for that of her captor. Brewster and Bragdon recognized the man as one of Mohammed's principal retainers, a fierce-looking fellow who had attracted more than usual attention on the day of the sheik's visit.

"For God's sake, don't kill her!" cried Brewster in agonized tones. There was a diabolical grin on the face of the Arab, who was about to shout back some defiant taunt when the unexpected happened.

The sharp crack of a gun sounded in the stern of Brewster's boat, and an unerring bullet sped straight for the big Arab's forehead.

It crashed between his eyes and death must have been instantaneous.   The knife flew from his hand, his body straightened and then collapsed, toppling over, not among his oarsmen, but across the gunwale of the craft. Before a hand could be lifted to prevent, the dead Arab and the girl were plunged into the sea.

A cry of horror went up from the Americans, and something surprisingly like a shout of triumph from the abductors.   Even as Brewster poised for the spring into the water a flying form shot past him and into the sea with a resounding splash.   The man that fired the shot had reckoned cleverly, and he was carrying out the final details of an inspired plan.   The Arab's position as he stood in the boat was such as to warrant the sailor's belief that he could fall no other way than forward, and that meant over the side of the boat. With all this clearly in mind he had shot straight and true and was on his way to the water almost as the two toppled overboard.

Monty Brewster was in the water an instant later, striking out for the spot where they had disappeared, a little to the left of the course in which his boat was running.   There was a rattle of firearms, with curses and cheers, but he paid no heed to these sounds. He was a length or two behind the sailor, praying with all his soul that one or the other might succeed in reaching the white robes that still kept the surface of the water. His crew was "backing water" and straining every muscle to bring the boat around sharp for the rescue.

The sailor's powerful strokes brought him to the spot first, but not in time to clutch the disappearing white robes. Just as he reached out an arm to grasp the form of the girl she went down. He did not hesitate a second but followed. Peggy had fallen from the dead Arab's embrace, and that worthy already was at the bottom of the sea. She was half conscious when the shot came, but the plunge into the cold water revived her. Her struggles were enough to keep her up for a few moments, but not long enough for the swimmers to reach her side. She felt herself going down and down, strangling, smothering, dying. Then something vise-like clutched her arm and she had the sensation of being jerked upward violently.

The sailor fought his way to the surface with the girl, and Brewster was at his side in an instant. Together they supported her until one of the boats came up, and they were drawn over the side to safety. By this time the abductors had scattered like sheep without a leader, and as there was no further object in pursuing them the little American fleet put back for the yacht in great haste. Peggy was quite conscious when carried aboard by the triumphant Brewster. The words he whispered to her as she lay in the bottom of the boat were enough to give her life.

The excitement on board the "Flitter" was boundless. Fear gave way to joy, and where despair had for a moment reigned supreme, there was now the most insane delight. Peggy was bundled below and into her berth, Dr. Lotless attending her, assisted by all the women on board. Brewster and the sailor, drenched but happy, were carried on the shoulders of enthusiastic supporters to a place where hot toddies were to be had before blankets.

"You have returned the favor, Conroy," said Brewster fervently, as he leaned across the heads of his bearers to shake hands with the sailor who was sharing the honors with him. Conroy was grinning from ear to ear as he sat perched on the shoulders of his shipmates. "I was luckier than I thought in saving your life that day."

"It wasn't anything, Mr. Brewster," said young Conroy. "I saw a chance to drop the big nigger, and then it was up to me to get her out of the water."

"You took a big risk, Conroy, but you made good with it. If it had not been for you, my boy, they might have got away with Miss Gray."

"Don't mention it, Mr. Brewster, it was nothing to do," protested Conroy in confusion. "I'd do anything in the world for you and for her."

"What is the adage about casting your bread upon the water and getting it back again?" asked "Rip" Van Winkle of Joe Bragdon as they jubilantly followed the procession below.

There was no more sleep on board that night. In fact the sun was not long in showing himself after the rescuers returned to the vessel. The daring attempt of Mohammed's emissaries was discussed without restraint, and every sailor had a story to tell of the pursuit and rescue. The event furnished conversational food for days and days among both the seamen and the passengers. Dan DeMille blamed himself relentlessly for sleeping through it all and moped for hours because he had lost a magnificent chance to "do something."

The next morning he proposed to hunt for the sheik, and offered to lead an assault in person. An investigation was made and government officials tried to call Mohammed to account, but he had fled to the desert and the search was fruitless.

Brewster refused to accept a share of the glory of Peggy's rescue, pushing Conroy forward as the real hero. But the sailor insisted that he could not have succeeded without help, —that he was completely exhausted when Monty came to the rescue. Peggy found it hard to thank him gently while her heart was so dangerously near the riot point, and her words of gratitude sounded pitifully weak and insufficient.

"It would have been the same had anybody else gone to her rescue," he mused dejectedly. "She cares for me with the devotion of a sister and that's all. Peggy, Peggy," he moaned, "if you could only love me, I'd— I'd—oh, well, there's no use thinking about it! She will love someone else, of course, and— and be happy, too. If she'd appear only one-tenth as grateful to me as to Conroy I'd be satisfied. He had the luck to be first, that's all, but God knows I tried to do it."

Mrs. Dan DeMille was keen enough to see

how the land lay, and she at once tried to set matters straight. She was far too clever to push her campaign ruthlessly, but laid her foundations and then built cunningly and securely with the most substantial material that came to hand from day to day. Her subjects were taking themselves too deeply to heart to appreciate interference on the part of an outsider, and Mrs. Dan was wise in the whims of love.

Peggy was not herself for several days after her experience, and the whole party felt a distinct relief when the yacht finally left the harbor and steamed off to the west. A cable-gram that came the day before may have had something to do with Brewster's depression, but he was not the sort to confess it. It was from Swearengen Jones, of Butte, Montana, and there was something sinister in the laconic admonition. It read:

"BREWSTER, U. S. CONSULATE, ALEXANDRIA.
  "Have a good time while good times last.
                                    "JONES."

His brain was almost bursting with the hopes and fears and uncertainties that crowded it far beyond its ordinary capacity. It had come to the point, it seemed to him, when the brains of a dozen men at least were required to operate the affairs that were surging into his alone. The mere fact that the end of his year was less than two months off, and that there was more or less uncertainty as to the character of the end, was sufficient cause for worry, but the new trouble was infinitely harder to endure. When he sat down to think over his financial enterprises his mind treacherously wandered off to Peggy Gray, and then everything was hopeless. He recalled the courage and confidence that had carried him to Barbara Drew with a declaration of love—to the stunning, worldly Barbara — and smiled bitterly when he saw how basely the two allies were deserting him in this hour of love for Peggy Gray. For some reason he had felt sure of Barbara; for another reason he saw no chance with Peggy. She was not the same sort—she was different. She was—well, she was Peggy.

Occasionally his reflections assumed the importance of calculations. His cruise was sure to cost $200,000, a princely sum, but not enough. Swearengen Jones and his cablegram did not awe him to a great extent. The spending of the million had become a mania with him now and he had no regard for consequences. His one desire, aside from Peggy, was to increase the cost of the cruise.

They were leaving Gibraltar when a new idea came into his troubled head.

He decided to change his plans and sail for the North Cape, thereby adding more than $30,000 to his credit.

CHAPTER XXVI

THE MUTINY

Monty was on deck when the inspiration seized him, and he lost no time in telling his guests, who were at breakfast. Although he had misgivings about their opinion of the scheme, he was not prepared for the ominous silence that followed his announcement.

"Are you in earnest, Mr. Brewster?" asked Captain Perry, who was the first of the company to recover from the surprise.

"Of course I am. I chartered this boat for four months with the privilege of another month. I can see no reason to prevent us from prolonging the trip." Monty's manner was full of self-assurance as he continued: "You people are so in the habit of protesting against every suggestion I make that you can't help doing it now."

"But, Monty," said Mrs. Dan, "what if your guests would rather go home?"

"Nonsense; you were asked for a five months' cruise. Besides, think of getting home in the middle of August, with everyone away. It would be like going to Philadelphia."

Brave as he was in the presence of his friends, in the privacy of his stateroom Monty gave way to the depression that was bearing down upon him. It was the hardest task of his life to go on with his scheme in the face of opposition. He knew that every man and woman on board was against the proposition, for his sake at least, and it was difficult to be arbitrary under the circumstances. Purposely he avoided Peggy all forenoon. His single glance at her face in the salon was enough to disturb him immeasurably.

The spirits of the crowd were subdued. The North Cape had charms, but the proclamation concerning it had been too sudden—had reversed too quickly the general expectation and desire. Many of the guests had plans at home for August, and even those who had none were satiated with excitement. During the morning they gathered in little knots to discuss the situation. They were all generous and each one was sure that he could cruise indefinitely, if on Monty's account the new voyage were not out of the question. They felt it their duty to take a desperate stand.

The half-hearted little gatherings resolved themselves into ominous groups and in the end there was a call for a general meeting in the main cabin. Captain Perry, the first mate, and the chief engineer were included in the call, but Montgomery Brewster was not to be admitted. Joe Bragdon loyally agreed to keep him engaged elsewhere while the meeting was in progress. The doors were locked and a cursory glance assured the chairman of the meeting, Dan DeMille, that no member of the party was missing save the devoted Bragdon. Captain Perry was plainly nervous and disturbed. The others were the victims of a suppressed energy that presaged subsequent eruptions.

"Captain Perry, we are assembled here for a purpose," said DeMille, clearing his throat three times. "First of all, as we understand it, you are the sailing master of this ship. In other words, you are, according to maritime law, the commander of this expedition. You alone can give orders to the sailors and you alone can clear a port. Mr. Brewster has no authority except that vested in a common employer. Am I correct?"

"Mr. DeMille, if Mr. Brewster instructs me to sail for the North Cape, I shall do so," said the captain, firmly. "This boat is his for the full term of the lease and I am engaged to sail her with my crew until the tenth of next September."

"We understand your position, captain, and I am sure you appreciate ours. It isn't that we want to end a very delightful cruise, but that we regard it as sheer folly for Mr. Brewster to extend the tour at such tremendous expense. He is—or was—a rich man, but it is impossible to ignore the fact that he is plunging much too heavily. In plain words, we want to keep him from spending more of his money on this cruise. Do you understand our position, Captain Perry?"

"Fully. I wish with all my soul that I could help you and him. My hands are tied by contract, however, much as I regret it at this moment."

"How does the crew feel about this additional trip, captain?" asked DeMille.

"They shipped for five months and will receive five months' pay. The men have been handsomely treated and they will stick to Mr. Brewster to the end," said the captain.

"There is no chance for a mutiny, then?" asked Smith regretfully. The captain gave him a hard look, but said nothing. Everybody seemed uncomfortable.

"Apparently the only way is the one sug-

gested by Mr. Smith this morning," said Mrs.
Dan, speaking for the women. "No one will
object, I am sure, if Captain Perry and his
chief officers are allowed to hear the plan."

"It is very necessary, in fact," said Mr.
Valentine. "We cannot proceed without them.
But they will agree with us, I am sure, that
it is wise."

An hour later the meeting broke up and the
conspirators made their way to the deck. It
was a strange fact that no one went alone.
They were in groups of three and four and the
mystery that hung about them was almost
perceptible. Not one was willing to face the
excited, buoyant Brewster without help; they
found strength and security in companionship.

Peggy was the one rebel against the conspiracy, and yet she knew that the others were
justified in the step they proposed to take.
She reluctantly joined them in the end, but felt
that she was the darkest traitor in the crowd.
Forgetting her own distress over the way in
which Monty was squandering his fortune, she
stood out the one defender of his rights until
the end and then admitted tearfully to Mrs.
DeMille that she had been "quite unreasonable" in doing so.

Alone in her stateroom after signing the

agreement, she wondered what he would think of her. She owed him so much that she at least should have stood by him. She felt that he would be conscious of this. How could she have turned against him? He would not understand—of course he would never understand. And he would hate her with the others—more than the others. It was all a wretched muddle and she could not see her way out of it.

Monty found his guests very difficult. They listened to his plans with but little interest, and he could not but see that they were uncomfortable. The situation was new to their experience, and they were under a strain. "They mope around like a lot of pouting boys and girls," he growled to himself. "But it's the North Cape now in spite of everything. I don't care if the whole crowd deserts me, my mind is made up."

Try as he would, he could not see Peggy alone. He had much that he wanted to say to her and he hungered for the consolation her approval would bring him, but she clung to Pettingill with a tenacity that was discouraging. The old feeling of jealousy that was connected with Como again disturbed him.

"She thinks that I am a hopeless, brainless

idiot," he said to himself. "And I don't blame her, either."

Just before nightfall he noticed that his friends were assembling in the bow. As he started to join the group "Subway" Smith and DeMille advanced to meet him. Some of the others were smiling a little sheepishly, but the two men were pictures of solemnity and decision.

"Monty," said DeMille steadily, "we have been conspiring against you and have decided that we sail for New York to-morrow morning."

Brewster stopped short and the expression on his face was one they never could forget. Bewilderment, uncertainty and pain succeeded each other like flashes of light. Not a word was spoken for several seconds. The red of humiliation slowly mounted to his cheeks, while in his eyes wavered the look of one who has been hunted down.

"You have decided?" he asked lifelessly, and more than one heart went out in pity to him.

"We hated to do it, Monty, but for your own sake there was no other way," said "Subway" Smith quickly. "We took a vote and there wasn't a dissenting voice."

"It is a plain case of mutiny, I take it," said Monty, utterly alone and heart-sick.

"It isn't necessary to tell you why we have. taken this step," said DeMille. "It is heartbreaking to oppose you at this stage of the game. You've been the best ever and——"

"Cut that," cried Monty, and his confidence in himself was fast returning. "This is no time to throw bouquets."

"We like you, Brewster." Mr. Valentine came to the chairman's assistance because the others had looked at him so appealingly. "We like you so well that we can't take the responsibility for your extravagance. It would disgrace us all."

"That side of the matter was never mentioned," cried Peggy indignantly, and then added with a catch in her voice, "We thought only of you."

"I appreciate your motives and I am grateful to you," said Monty. "I am more sorry than I can tell you that the cruise must end in this way, but I too have decided. The yacht will take you to some point where you can catch a steamer to New York. I shall secure passage for the entire party and very soon you will be at home. Captain Perry, will you oblige me by making at once for any port that my guests

may agree upon?'' He was turning away deliberately when "Subway" Smith detained him.

"What do you mean by getting a steamer to
New York? Isn't the 'Flitter' good enough?''
he asked.

"The 'Flitter' is not going to New York just
now," answered Brewster firmly, "notwithstanding your ultimatum. She is going to
take *me* to the North Cape.''

CHAPTER XXVII

A FAIR TRAITOR

"Now will you be good?" cried Reggie Vanderpool to DeMille as Monty went down the companionway. The remark was precisely what was needed, for the pent-up feelings of the entire company were now poured forth upon the unfortunate young man. "Subway" Smith was for hanging him to the yard arm, and the denunciation of the others was so decisive that Reggie sought refuge in the chart house. But the atmosphere had been materially cleared and the leaders of the mutiny were in a position to go into executive session and consider the matter. The women waited on deck while the meeting lasted. They were unanimous in the opinion that the affair had been badly managed.

"They should have offered to stay by the ship providing Monty would let Mr. DeMille manage the cruise," said Miss Valentine. "That would have been a concession and at the same time it would have put the cruise on an economical basis."

"In other words you will accept a man's

invitation to dinner if he will allow you to order it and invite the other guests," said Peggy, who was quick to defend Monty.

"Well that would be better than helping to eat up every bit of food he possessed." But Miss Valentine always avoided argument when she could and gave this as a parting thrust before she walked away.

"There must be something more than we know about in Monty's extravagance," said Mrs. Dan. "He isn't the kind of man to squander his last penny without having something left to show for it. There must be method in his madness."

"He has done it for us," said Peggy. "He has devoted himself all along to giving us a good time and now we are showing our gratitude."

Further discussion was prevented by the appearance of the conspiring committee and the whole company was summoned to hear DeMille's report as chairman.

"We have found a solution of our difficulties," he began, and his manner was so jubilant that everyone became hopeful. "It is desperate but I think it will be effective. Monty has given us the privilege of leaving the yacht at any port where we can take a steamer to New York. Now, my suggestion is that we select the most convenient place for all of us, and obviously there is nothing quite so convenient as Boston.''

"Dan DeMille, you are quite foolish,'' cried his wife. "Who ever conceived such a ridiculous idea?''

"Captain Perry has his instructions,'' continued DeMille, turning to the captain. "Are we not acting along the lines marked out by Brewster himself?''

"I will sail for Boston if you say the word,'' said the thoughtful captain. "But he is sure to countermand such an order.''

"He won't be able to, captain,'' cried "Subway'' Smith, who had for some time been eager to join in the conversation. "This is a genuine, dyed-in-the-wool mutiny and we expect to carry out the original plan, which was to put Mr. Brewster in irons, until we are safe from all opposition.''

"He is my friend, Mr. Smith, and at least it is my duty to protect him from any indignity,'' said the captain, stiffly.

"You make for Boston, my dear captain, and we'll do the rest,'' said DeMille. "Mr. Brewster can't countermand your orders unless he sees you in person. We'll see to it that he has no chance to talk to you until we are in sight of Boston Harbor.''

The captain looked doubtful and shook his head as he walked away. At heart he was with the mutineers and his mind was made up to assist them as long as it was possible to do so without violating his obligations to Brewster. He felt guilty, however, in surreptitiously giving the order to clear for Boston at daybreak. The chief officers were let into the secret, but the sailors were kept in darkness regarding the destination of the "Flitter."

Montgomery Brewster's guests were immensely pleased with the scheme, although they were dubious about the outcome. Mrs. Dan regretted her hasty comment on the plan and entered into the plot with eagerness. In accordance with plans decided upon by the mutineers, Monty's stateroom door was guarded through the night by two of the men. The next morning as he emerged from his room, he was met by "Subway" Smith and Dan DeMille.

"Good morning," was his greeting. "How's the weather to-day?"

"Bully," answered DeMille. "By the way, you are going to have breakfast in your room, old man."

Brewster unsuspectingly led the way into his stateroom, the two following.

"What's the mystery?" he demanded.

"We've been deputized to do some very nasty work," said "Subway" as he turned the key in the door. "We are here to tell you what port we have chosen."

"It's awfully good of you to tell me."

"Yes, isn't it? But we have studied up on the chivalrous treatment of prisoners. We have decided on Boston."

"Is there a Boston on this side of the water?" asked Monty in mild surprise.

"No; there is only one Boston in the universe, so far as we know. It is a large body of intellect surrounded by the rest of the world."

"What the devil are you talking about? You don't mean Boston, Massachusetts?" cried Monty, leaping to his feet.

"Precisely. That's the port for us and you told us to choose for ourselves," said Smith.

"Well, I won't have it, that's all," exclaimed Brewster, indignantly. "Captain Perry takes orders from me and from no one else."

"He already has his orders," said DeMille, smiling mysteriously.

"I'll see about that. Brewster sprang to the door. It was locked and the key was in "Subway" Smith's pocket. With an impatient exclamation he turned and pressed an electric button.

"It won't ring, Monty," explained "Subway." "The wire has been cut. Now, be cool for a minute or two and we'll talk it over."

Brewster stormed for five minutes, the "delegation" sitting calmly by, smiling with exasperating confidence. At last he calmed down and in terms of reason demanded an explanation. He was given to understand that the yacht would sail for Boston and that he would be kept a prisoner for the entire voyage unless he submitted to the will of the majority.

Brewster listened darkly to the proclamation. He saw that they had gained the upper hand by a clever ruse, and that only strategy on his part could outwit them. It was out of the question for him to submit to them now that the controversy had assumed the dignity of a struggle.

"But you will be reasonable, won't you?" asked DeMille, anxiously.

"I intend to fight it out to the bitter end," said Brewster, his eyes flashing. "At present I am your prisoner, but it is a long way to Boston."

For three days and two nights the "Flitter" steamed westward into the Atlantic, with her temporary owner locked into his stateroom. The confinement was irksome, but he rather liked the sensation of being interested in something besides money. He frequently laughed to himself over the absurdity of the situation. His enemies were friends, true and devoted; his gaolers were relentless but they were considerate. The original order that he should be guarded by one man was violated on the first day. There were times when his guard numbered at least ten persons and some of them served tea and begged him to listen to reason.

"It is difficult not to listen," he said fiercely. "It's like holding a man down and then asking him to be quiet. But my time is coming."

"Revenge will be his!" exclaimed Mrs. Dan, tragically.

"You might have your term shortened on account of good conduct if you would only behave," suggested Peggy, whose reserve was beginning to soften. "Please be good and give in."

"I haven't been happier during the whole cruise," said Monty. "On deck I wouldn't be noticed, but here I am quite the whole thing. Besides I can get out whenever I feel like it."

"I have a thousand dollars which says you can't," said DeMille, and Monty snapped him up so eagerly that he added, "that you can't get out of your own accord."

Monty acceded to the condition and offered odds on the proposition to the others, but there were no takers.

"That settles it," he smiled grimly to himself. "I can make a thousand dollars by staying here and I can't afford to escape."

On the third day of Monty's imprisonment the "Flitter" began to roll heavily. At first he gloated over the discomfort of his guards who obviously did not like to stay below. "Subway" Smith and Bragdon were on duty and neither was famous as a good sailor. When Monty lighted his pipe there was consternation and "Subway" rushed on deck.

"*You* are a brave man, Joe," Monty said to the other and blew a cloud of smoke in his direction. "I knew you would stick to your post. You wouldn't leave it even if the ship should go down."

Bragdon had reached the stage where he dared not speak and was busying himself try-

ing to "breathe with the motion of the boat"
as he had called it.

"By Gad," continued Monty, relentlessly.
"This smoke is getting thick. Some of this
toilet water might help if I sprinkled it about."

One whiff of the sweet-smelling cologne
was enough for Bragdon and he bolted up the
companionway, leaving the stateroom door
wide open and the prisoner free to go where he
pleased. Monty's first impulse was to follow
but he checked himself on the threshold.

"Damn that bet with DeMille," he said to
himself, and added aloud to the fleeing guard,
"The key, Joe, I dare you to come back and
get it!"

But Bragdon was beyond recall and Monty
locked the door on the inside and passed the
key through the ventilator.

On deck a small part of the company braved
the spray in the lee of the deck house, but the
others had long since gone below. The boat
was pitching furiously in the ugliest sea it
had encountered, and there was anxiety underneath Captain Perry's mask of unconcern.
DeMille and Dr. Lotless talked in the senseless
way men have when they try to conceal their
nervousness. But the women did not respond;
they were in no mood for conversation.

Only one of them was quite oblivious to personal discomfort and danger. Peggy Gray was thinking of the prisoner below. In a reflection of her own terror, she pictured him crouching in the little stateroom, like a doomed criminal awaiting execution, alone, neglected, forgotten, unpitied. At first she pleaded with the men for his release, but they insisted upon waiting in the hope that a scare might bring him to his senses. Peggy saw that no help was to be secured from the other women, much as they might care for Brewster's peace of mind and safety. Her heart was bitter toward everyone responsible for the situation, and there was dark rebellion in her soul. It culminated finally in a resolve to release Monty Brewster at any cost.

With difficulty she made her way to the stateroom door, clinging to supports at times and then plunging violently away from them. For some minutes she listened, frantically clutching Brewster's door and the wall-rail. There was no guard, and the tumult of the sea drowned every sound within. Her imagination ran riot when her repeated calls were not answered.

"Monty, Monty," she cried, pounding wildly on the door.

"Who is it?   What is the trouble?" came in muffled tones from within, and Peggy breathed a prayer of thanks.   Just then she discovered the key which Monty had dropped and quickly opened the door, expecting to find him cowering with fear.   But the picture was different. The prisoner was seated on the divan, propped up with many pillows and reading with the aid of an electric light "The Intrusions of Peggy."

CHAPTER XXVIII

A CATASTROPHE

"Oh!" was Peggy's only exclamation, and there was a shadow of disappointment in her eyes.

"Come in, Peggy, and I'll read aloud," was Monty's cheerful greeting as he stood before her.

"No, I must go," said Peggy, confusedly. "I thought you might be nervous about the storm—and—"

"And you came to let me out?" Monty had never been so happy.

"Yes, and I don't care what the others say. I thought you were suffering—" But at that moment the boat gave a lurch which threw her across the threshold into Monty's arms. They crashed against the wall, and he held her a moment and forgot the storm. When she drew away from him she showed him the open door and freedom. She could not speak.

"Where are the others?" he asked, bracing himself in the doorway.

"Oh, Monty," she cried, "we must not go to them. They will think me a traitor."

"Why were you a traitor, Peggy?" he demanded, turning toward her suddenly.

"Oh—oh, because it seemed so cruel to keep you locked up through the storm," she answered, blushing.

"And there was no other reason?" he persisted.

"Don't, please don't!" she cried, piteously, and he misunderstood her emotion. It was clear that she was merely sorry for him.

"Never mind, Peggy, it's all right. You stood by me and I'll stand by you. Come on; we'll face the mob and I'll do the fighting."

Together they made their way into the presence of the mutineers, who were crowded into the main cabin.

"Well, here's a conspiracy," cried Dan DeMille, but there was no anger in his voice. "How did you escape? I was just thinking of unlocking your door, Monty, but the key seemed to be missing."

Peggy displayed it triumphantly.

"By Jove," cried Dan. "This is rank treachery. Who was on guard?"

A steward rushing through the cabin at this moment in answer to frantic calls from Bragdon furnished an eloquent reply to the question.

"It was simple," said Monty. "The guards deserted their post and left the key behind."

"Then it is up to me to pay you a thousand dollars."

"Not at all," protested Monty, taken aback "I did not escape of my own accord. I had help. The money is yours. And now that I am free," he added, quietly, "let me say that this boat does not go to Boston."

"Just what I expected," cried Vanderpool.

"She's going straight to New York!" declared Monty. The words were hardly uttered when a heavy sea sent him sprawling across the cabin and he concluded, "or to the bottom."

"Not so bad as that," said Captain Perry, whose entrance had been somewhat hastened by the lurch of the boat. "But until this blows over I must keep you below." He laughed but he saw they were not deceived. "The seas are pretty heavy and the decks are being holystoned for nothing, but I wouldn't like to have any of you washed overboard by mistake."

The hatches were battened down, and it was a sorry company that tried to while away the evening in the main cabin. Monty's chaffing about the advantages of the North Cape over the stormy Atlantic was not calculated to raise the drooping spirits, and it was very early when he and his shattered guests turned in. There was little sleep on board the "Flitter" that night. Even if it had been easy to forget the danger, the creaking of the ship and the incessant roar of the water were enough for wakefulness. With each lurch of the boat it seemed more incredible that it could endure. It was such a mite of a thing to meet so furious an attack. As it rose on the wave to pause in terror on its crest before sinking shivering into the trough, it made the breath come short and the heart stand still. Through the night the fragile little craft fought its lonely way, bravely ignoring its own weakness and the infinite strength of its enemy. To the captain, lashed to the bridge, there were hours of grave anxiety—hours when he feared each wave as it approached, and wondered what new damage it had done as it receded. As the wind increased toward morning he felt a sickening certainty that the brave little boat was beaten. Somehow she seemed to lose courage, to waver a bit and almost give up the fight. He watched her miserably as the dismal dawn came up out of the sea. Yet it was not until seven o'clock that the crash came, which shook the passengers out of their berths and filled them with shivering terror. The whirling of the broken shaft seemed to consume the ship. In every cabin it spoke with horrible vividness of disaster. The clamor of voices and the rush of many feet, which followed, meant but one thing. Almost instantly the machinery was stopped—an ominous silence in the midst of the dull roar of the water and the cry of the wind.

It was a terrified crowd that quickly gathered in the main cabin, but it was a brave one. There were no cries and few tears. They expected anything and were ready for the worst, but they would not show the white feather. It was Mrs. Dan who broke the tension. "I made sure of my pearls," she said; "I thought they would be appreciated at the bottom of the sea."

Brewster came in upon their laughter. "I like your nerve, people," he exclaimed, "you are all right. It won't be so bad now. The wind has dropped."

Long afterward when they talked the matter over, DeMille claimed that the only thing that bothered him that night was the effort to decide whether the club of which he and Monty were members would put in the main hallway two black-bordered cards, each bearing a name, or only one with both names. Mr. Valentine regretted that he had gone on for years paying life insurance premiums when now his only relatives were on the boat and would die with him.

The captain, looking pretty rocky after his twenty-hour vigil, summoned his chief. "We're in a bad hole, Mr. Brewster," he said when they were alone, "and no mistake. A broken shaft and this weather make a pretty poor combination."

"Is there no chance of making a port for repairs?"

"I don't see it, sir. It looks like a long pull."

"We are way off our course, I suppose?" and Monty's coolness won Captain Perry's admiration.

"I can't tell just how much until I get the sun, but this wind is hell. I suspect we've drifted pretty far."

"Come and get some coffee, captain. While the storm lasts the only thing to do is to cheer up the women and trust to luck."

"You are the nerviest mate I ever shipped with, Mr. Brewster," and the captain's hand gripped Monty's in a way that meant things. It was a tribute he appreciated.

During the day Monty devoted himself to his guests, and at the first sign of pensiveness he was ready with a jest or a story. But he did it all with a tact that inspired the crowd as a whole with hope, and no one suspected that he himself was not cheerful. For Peggy Gray there was a special tenderness, and he made up his mind that if things should go wrong he would tell her that he loved her.

"It could do no harm," he thought to himself, "and I want her to know."

Toward night the worst was over. The sea had gone down and the hatches were opened for a while to admit air, though it was still too rough to venture out. The next morning was bright and clear. When the company gathered on deck the havoc created by the storm was apparent. Two of the boats had been completely carried away and the launch was rendered useless by a large hole in the stern.

"You don't mean to say that we will drift about until the repairs can be made?" asked Mrs. Dan in alarm.

"We are three hundred miles off the course already," explained Monty, "and it will be pretty slow traveling under sail."

It was decided to make for the Canary Islands, where repairs could be made and the voyage resumed. But where the wind had raged a few days before, it had now disappeared altogether, and for a week the "Flitter" tossed about absolutely unable to make head-way. The first of August had arrived and Monty himself was beginning to be nervous. With the fatal day not quite two months away, things began to look serious. Over one hundred thousand dollars would remain after he had settled the expenses of the cruise, and he was helplessly drifting in mid-ocean. Even if the necessary repairs could be made promptly, it would take the "Flitter" fourteen days to sail from the Canaries to New York. Figure as hard as he could he saw no way out of the unfortunate situation. Two days more elapsed and still no sign of a breeze. He made sure that September 23d would find him still drift-ing and still in possession of one hundred thousand superfluous dollars.

At the end of ten days the yacht had pro-gressed but two hundred miles and Monty was beginning to plan the rest of his existence on a capital of $100,000. He had given up all hope of the Sedgwick legacy and was trying to be resigned to his fate, when a tramp steamer was suddenly sighted. Brewster ordered the man on watch to fly a flag of distress. Then he reported to the captain and told what he had done. With a bound the captain rushed on deck and tore the flag from the sailor's hand.

"That was my order," said Monty, nettled at the captain's manner.

"You want them to get a line on us and claim salvage, do you?"

"What do you mean?"

"If they get a line on us in response to that flag they will claim the entire value of the ship as salvage. You want to spend another $200,000 on this boat?"

"I didn't understand," said Monty, sheepishly. "But for God's sake, fix it up somehow. Can't they tow us? I'll pay for it."

Communication was slow, but after an apparently endless amount of signaling, the captain finally announced that the freight steamer was bound for Southampton and would tow the "Flitter" to that point for a price.

"Back to Southampton!" groaned Monty. "That means months before we get back to New York."

"He says he can get us to Southampton in ten days," interrupted the captain.

"I can do it, I can do it," he cried, to the consternation of his guests who wondered if his mind were affected. "If he'll land us in Southampton by the 27th, I'll pay him up to one hundred thousand dollars."

CHAPTER XXIX

THE PRODIGAL'S RETURN

After what seemed an age to Monty, the "Flitter," in tow of the freighter "Glencoe," arrived at Southampton. The captain of the freight boat was a thrifty Scotchman whose ship was traveling with a light cargo and he was not, therefore, averse to taking on a tow. But the thought of salvage had caused him to ask a high price for the service and Monty, after a futile attempt at bargaining, had agreed. The price was fifty thousand dollars, and the young man believed more than ever that everything was ruled by a wise Providence, which had not deserted him. His guests were heart-sick when they heard the figure, but were as happy as Monty at the prospect of reaching land again.

The "Glencoe" made several stops before Southampton was finally reached on the 28th of August, but when the English coast was sighted everyone was too eager to go ashore to begrudge the extra day. Dan DeMille asked the entire party to become his guests for a week's shooting trip in Scotland, but Monty vetoed the plan in the most decided manner.

"We sail for New York on the fastest boat," said Monty, and hurried off to learn the sailings and book his party. The first boat was to sail on the 30th and he could only secure accommodations for twelve of his guests. The rest were obliged to follow a week later. This was readily agreed to and Bragdon was left to see to the necessary repairs on the "Flitter" and arrange for her homeward voyage. Monty gave Bragdon fifteen thousand dollars for this purpose and extracted a solemn promise that the entire amount would be used.

"But it won't cost half of this," protested Bragdon

"You will have to give these people a good time during the week and—well—you have promised that I shall never see another penny of it. Some day you'll know why I do this," and Monty felt easier when his friend agreed to abide by his wishes.

He discharged the "Flitter's" crew, with five months' pay and the reward promised on the night of Peggy's rescue, which was productive of touching emotions. Captain Perry and his officers never forgot the farewell of

the prodigal, nor could they hide the regret
that marked their weather-beaten faces.

Plans to dispose of his household goods and
the balance of his cash in the short time that
would be left after he arrived in New York
occupied Monty's attention, and most men
would have given up the scheme as hopeless.
But he did not despair. He was still game,
and he prepared for the final plunge with grim
determination.

"There should have been a clause in Jones's
conditions about 'weather permitting,' " he
said to himself. "A shipwrecked mariner
should not be expected to spend a million
dollars."

The division of the party for the two sailings
was tactfully arranged by Mrs. DeMille. The
Valentines chaperoned the "second table" as
"Subway" Smith called those who were to take
the later boat, and she herself looked after the
first lot. Peggy Gray and Monty Brewster
were in the DeMille party. The three days in
England were marked by unparalleled extravagance on Monty's part. One of the local
hotels was subsidized for a week, although the
party only stayed for luncheon, and the Cecil
in London was a gainer by several thousand
dollars for the brief stop there. It was a

careworn little band that took Monty's special
train for Southampton and embarked two days
later. The "rest cure" that followed was
welcome to all of them and Brewster was
especially glad that his race was almost
run.

Swiftly and steadily the liner cut down the
leagues that separated her from New York.
Fair weather and fair cheer marked her course,
and the soft, balmy nights were like seasons
of fairyland. Monty was cherishing in his
heart the hope inspired by Peggy's action on
the night of the storm. Somehow it brought
a small ray of light to his clouded understand-
ing and he found joy in keeping the flame
alive religiously if somewhat doubtfully. His
eyes followed her constantly, searching for the
encouragement that the very blindness of love
had hidden from him, forever tormenting himself with fears and hopes and fears again. Her
happiness and vivacity puzzled him—he was
often annoyed, he was now and then seriously
mystified.

Four days out from New York, then three
days, then two days, and then Brewster began
to feel the beginning of the final whirlwind in
profligacy clouding him oppressively, ominously, unkindly. Down in his state room he

drew new estimates, new calculations, and tried
to balance the old ones so that they appeared
in the light most favorable to his designs.
Going over the statistics carefully, he estimated
that the cruise, including the repairs and the
return of the yacht to New York, would cost
him $210,000 in round figures.   One hundred
and thirty-three days marked the length of the
voyage when reckoned by time and, as near as
he could get at it, the expense had averaged
$1,580 a day.   According to the contract, he
was to pay for the yacht, exclusive of the
cuisine and personal service.   And he had
found it simple enough to spend the remaining
$1,080.   There were days, of course, when
fully $5,000 disappeared, and there were others
on which he spent much less than $1,000, but
the average was secure.   Taking everything
into consideration, Brewster found that his
fortune had dwindled to a few paltry thousands
in addition to the proceeds which would come
to him from the sale of his furniture.   On the
whole he was satisfied.

The landing in New York and the separation
which followed were not entirely merry.   Every
discomfort was forgotten and the travelers only
knew that the most wonderful cruise since that
of the ark had come to an end.   There was not

one who would not have been glad to begin it again the next day.

Immediately after the landing Brewster and Gardner were busy with the details of settlement. After clearing up all of the obligations arising from the cruise, they felt the appropriateness of a season of reflection. It was a difficult moment—a moment when undelivered reproofs were in the air. But Gardner seemed much the more melancholy of the two.

Piles of newspapers lay scattered about the floor of the room in which they sat. Every one of them contained sensational stories of the prodigal's trip, with pictures, incidents and predictions. Monty was pained, humiliated and resentful, but he was honest enough to admit the justification of much that was said of him. He read bits of it here and there and then threw the papers aside hopelessly. In a few weeks they would tell another story, and quite as emphatically.

"The worst of it, Monty, is that you are the next thing to being a poor man," groaned Gardner. "I've done my best to economize for you here at home, as you'll see by these figures, but **nothing** could possibly balance the extravagances of this voyage. They are simply appalling."

With the condemnation of his friends ringing in his troubled brain, with the sneers of acquaintances to distress his pride, with the jibes of the comic papers to torture him remorselessly, Brewster was fast becoming the most miserable man in New York. Friends of former days gave him the cut direct, clubmen ignored him or scorned him openly, women chilled him with the iciness of unspoken reproof, and all the world was hung with shadows. The doggedness of despair kept him up, but the strain that pulled down on him was so relentless that the struggle was losing its equality. He had not expected such a home-coming.

Compared with his former self, Monty was now almost a physical wreck, haggard, thin and defiant, a shadow of the once debonair young New Yorker, an object of pity and scorn. Ashamed and despairing, he had almost lacked the courage to face Mrs. Gray. The consolation he once gained through her he now denied himself and his suffering, peculiar as it was, was very real. In absolute recklessness he gave dinner after dinner, party after party, all on a most lavish scale, many of his guests laughing at him openly while they enjoyed his hospitality. The real friends remonstrated, pleaded, did everything within their power to check his awful rush to poverty, but without success; he was not to be stopped.

At last the furniture began to go, then the plate, then all the priceless bric-à-brac. Piece by piece it disappeared until the apartments were empty and he had squandered almost all of the $40,350 arising from the sales. The servants were paid off, the apartments relinquished, and he was beginning to know what it meant to be "on his uppers." At the banks he ascertained that the interest on his moneys amounted to $19,140.86. A week before the 23d of September, the whole million was gone, including the amounts won in Lumber and Fuel and other luckless enterprises. He still had about $17,000 of his interest money in the banks, but he had a billion pangs in his heart— the interest on his improvidence.

He found some delight in the discovery that the servants had robbed him of not less than $3,500 worth of his belongings, including the Christmas presents that he in honor could not have sold. His only encouragement came from Grant and Ripley, the lawyers. They inspired confidence in his lagging brain by urging him on to the end, promising brightness thereafter. Swearengen Jones was as mute as the mountains in which he lived. There was

no word from him, there was no assurance that
he would approve of what had been done to
obliterate Edwin Peter Brewster's legacy.

Dan DeMille and his wife implored Monty to
come with them to the mountains before his
substance was gone completely. The former
offered him money, employment, rest and
security if he would abandon the course he was
pursuing. Up in Fortieth Street Peggy Gray
was grieving her heart out and he knew it.
Two or three of those whom he had considered
friends refused to recognize him in the street
in this last trying week, and it did not even
interest him to learn that Miss Barbara Drew
was to become a duchess before the winter was
gone. Yet he found some satisfaction in the
report that one Hampton of Chicago had long
since been dropped out of the race.

One day he implored the faithful Bragdon to
steal the Boston terriers. He could not and
would not sell them and he dared not give them
away. Bragdon dejectedly appropriated the
dogs and Brewster announced that some day
he would offer a reward for their return and
"no questions asked."

He took a suite of rooms in a small hotel
and was feverishly planning the overthrow of
the last torturing thousands. Bragdon lived

with him and the "Little Sons of the Rich"
stood loyally ready to help him when he
uttered the first cry of want But even this
establishment had to be abandoned at last.
The old rooms in Fortieth Street were still
open to him and though he quailed at the
thought of making them a refuge, he faced the
ordeal in the spirit of a martyr.

CHAPTER XXX

THE PROMISE OF THRIFT

"Monty, you are breaking my heart," was the first and only appeal Mrs. Gray ever made to him. It was two days before the twenty-third and it did not come until after the "second-hand store" men had driven away from her door with the bulk of his clothing in their wagon. She and Peggy had seen little of Brewster, and his nervous restlessness alarmed them His return was the talk of the town. Men tried to shun him, but he persistently wasted some portion of his fortune on his unwilling subjects. When he gave $5,000 in cash to a Home for Newsboys, even his friends jumped to the conclusion that he was mad. It was his only gift to charity and he excused his motive in giving at this time by recalling Sedgwick's injunction to "give sparingly to charity." Everything was gone from his thoughts but the overpowering eagerness to get rid of a few troublesome thousands. He felt like an outcast, a pariah, a hated object that infected everyone with whom he came in contact. Sleep was almost impossible, eating was a farce; he gave elaborate suppers which he did not touch. Already his best friends were discussing the advisability of putting him in a sanitarium where his mind might be preserved. His case was looked upon as peculiar in the history of mankind; no writer could find a parallel, no one could imagine a comparison.

Mrs. Gray met him in the hallway of her home as he was nervously pocketing the $60 he had received in payment for his clothes. Her face was like that of a ghost. He tried to answer her reproof, but the words would not come, and he fled to his room, locking the door after him. He was at work there on the transaction that was to record the total disappearance of Edwin Brewster's million—his final report to Swearengen Jones, executor of James Sedgwick's will. On the floor were bundles of packages, carefully wrapped and tied, and on the table was the long sheet of white paper on which the report was being drawn. The packages contained receipts— thousands upon thousands of them—for the dollars he had spent in less than a year. They were there for the inspection of Swearengen Jones, faithfully and honorably kept—as if the old westerner would go over in detail the countless documents.

He had the accounts balanced up to the hour. On the long sheet lay the record of his ruthlessness, the epitaph of a million. In his pocket was exactly $79.08. This was to last him for less than forty-eight hours and—then it would go to join the rest. It was his plan to visit Grant & Ripley on the afternoon of the twenty-second and to read the report to them, in anticipation of the meeting with Jones on the day following.

Just before noon, after his encounter with Mrs. Gray, he came down stairs and boldly, for the first time in days, sought out Peggy. There was the old smile in his eyes and the old heartiness in his voice when he came upon her in the library. She was not reading. Books, pleasures and all the joys of life had fled from her mind and she thought only of the disaster that was coming to the boy she had always loved. His heart smote him as he looked into the deep, somber, frightened eyes, running over with love and fear for him.

"Peggy, do you think I'm worth anything more from your mother? Do you think she will ask me to live here any longer?" he asked, steadily, taking her hand in his. Hers was cold, his as hot as fire. "You know what you said away off yonder somewhere, that she'd let me live here if I deserved it. I am a pauper, Peggy, and I'm afraid I'll—I may have to get down to drudgery again. Will she turn me out? You know I must have somewhere to live. Shall it be the poorhouse? Do you remember saying one day that I'd end in the poorhouse?"

She was looking into his eyes, dreading what might be seen in them. But there was no gleam of insanity there, there was no fever; instead there was the quiet smile of the man who is satisfied with himself and the world. His voice bore traces of emotion, but it was the voice of one who has perfect control of his wits.

"Is it all—gone, Monty?" she asked, almost in a whisper.

"Here is the residue of my estate," he said, opening his purse with steady fingers. "I'm back to where I left off a year ago. The million is gone and my wings are clipped." Her face was white, her heart was in the clutch of ice. How could he be so calm about it when for him she was suffering such agony? Twice she started to speak, but her voice failed her. She turned slowly and walked to the window, keeping her back to the man who smiled so sadly and yet so heartlessly.

"I didn't want the million, Peggy," he went on. "You think as the rest do, I know, that I was a fool to act as I did. It would be rank idiocy on my part to blame you any more than the others for thinking as you do. Appearances are against me, the proof is overwhelming A year ago I was called a man, to-day they are stripping me of every claim to that distinction. The world says I am a fool, a dolt, almost a criminal—but no one believes I am a man. Peggy, will you feel better toward me if I tell you that I am going to begin life all over again? It will be a new Monty Brewster that starts out again in a few days, or, if you will, it shall be the old one— the Monty you once knew."

"The old Monty?" she murmured softly, dreamily. "It would be good to see him—so much better than to see the Monty of the last year."

"And, in spite of all I have done, Peggy, you will stand by me? You won't desert me like the rest? You'll be the same Peggy of the other days?" he cried, his calmness breaking down.

"How can you ask? Why should you doubt me?"

For a moment they stood silent, each looking into the heart of the other, each seeing the beginning of a new day.

"Child," his voice trembled dangerously, "I—I wonder if you care enough for me to—to—" but he could only look the question.

"To start all over again with you?" she whispered.

"Yes—to trust yourself to the prodigal who has returned. Without you, child, all the rest would be as the husks. Peggy, I want you—you! You *do* love me—I can see it in your eyes, I can feel it in your presence."

"How long you have been in realizing it," she said pensively as she stretched out her arms to him. For many minutes he held her close, finding a beautiful peace in the world again.

"How long have you really cared?" he asked in a whisper.

"Always, Monty; all my life."

"And I too, child, all my life. I know it now; I've known it for months. Oh, what a fool I was to have wasted all this love of yours and all this love of mine. But I'll not be a profligate in love, Peggy. I'll not squander an atom of it, dear, not as long as I live."

"And we will build a greater love, Monty, as we build the new life together. We never can be poor while we have love as a treasure."

"You won't mind being poor with me?" he asked.

"I can't be poor with you," she said simply.

"And I might have let all this escape me," he cried fervently. "Listen, Peggy—we will start together, you as my wife and my fortune. You shall be all that is left to me of the past. Will you marry me the day after to-morrow? Don't say no, dearest. I want to begin on that day. At seven in the morning, dear? Don't you see how good the start will be?"

And he pleaded so ardently and so earnestly that he won his point even though it grew out of a whim that she could not then understand. She was not to learn until afterward his object in having the marriage take place on the morning of September 23d, two hours before the time set for the turning over of the Sedgwick millions. If all went well they would be Brewster's millions before twelve o'clock, and Peggy's life of poverty would cover no more than three hours of time. She believed him worth a lifetime of poverty. So they would start the new life with but one possession—love.

Peggy rebelled against his desire to spend the seventy dollars that still remained, but he was firm in his determination. They would dine and drive together and see all of the old life that was left—on seventy dollars. Then on the next day they would start all over again. There was one rude moment of dismay when it occurred to him that Peggy might be considered an "asset" if she became his wife before nine o'clock. But he realized at once that it was only demanded of him that he be penniless and that he possess no object that had been acquired through the medium of Edwin Peter Brewster's money. Surely this wife who was not to come to him until his last dollar was gone could not be the product of an old man's legacy. But so careful was he in regard to the transaction that he decided to borrow money of Joe Bragdon to buy the license and to pay the minister's fee. Not only would he be penniless on the day of settlement, but he would be in debt. So changed was the color of the world to him now that even the failure to win Sedgwick's millions could not crush out the new life and the new joy that had come to him with the winning of Peggy Gray.

CHAPTER XXXI

HOW THE MILLION DISAPPEARED

Soon after noon on the 22d of September, Monty folded his report to Swearengen Jones, stuck it into his pocket and sallied forth. A parcel delivery wagon had carried off a mysterious bundle a few minutes before. Mrs. Gray could not conceal her wonder but Brewster's answers to her questions threw little light on the mystery. He could not tell her the big bundle contained the receipts that were to prove his sincerity when the time came to settle with Mr. Jones. Brewster had used his own form of receipt for every purchase. The little stub receipt books had been made to order for him and not only he but every person in his employ carried one everywhere. No matter how trivial the purchase, the person who received a dollar of Brewster's money signed a receipt for the amount. Newsboys and bootblacks were the only beings who escaped the formality; tips to waiters, porters, cabbies, etc., were recorded and afterward put into a class by themselves. Receipts for the few dollars remaining in his possession were to be turned over on the morning of the 23d and the general report was not to be completed until 9 o'clock on that day.

He kissed Peggy good-bye, told her to be ready for a drive at 4 o'clock, and then went off to find Joe Bragdon and Elon Gardner. They met him by appointment and to them he confided his design to be married on the following day.

"You can't afford it, Monty," exploded Joe, fearlessly. "Peggy is too good a girl. By gad, it isn't fair to her."

"We have agreed to begin life to-morrow. Wait and see the result. I think it will surprise you. Incidentally it is up to me to get the license to-day and to engage a minister's services. It's going to be quiet, you know. Joe, you can be my best man if you like and, Gardie, I'll expect you to sign your name as one of the witnesses. To-morrow evening we'll have supper at Mrs. Gray's and 'among those present' will not comprise a very large list, I assure you. But we'll talk about that later on. Just now I want to ask you fellows to lend me enough money to get the license and pay the preacher. I'll return it to-morrow afternoon."

"Well, I'm damned," exclaimed Gardner,

utterly dumbfounded by the nerve of the man. But they went with him to get the license and Bragdon paid for it. Gardner promised to have the minister at the Gray house the next morning. Monty's other request—made in deep seriousness—was that Peggy was not to be told of the little transaction in which the license and the minister figured so prominently. He then hurried off to the office of Grant & Ripley. The bundles of receipts had preceded him.

"Has Jones arrived in town?" was his first anxious question after the greetings.

"He is not registered at any of the hotels," responded Mr. Grant, and Brewster did not see the troubled look that passed over his face.

"He'll show up to-night, I presume," said he, complacently. The lawyers did not tell him that all the telegrams they had sent to Swearengen Jones in the past two weeks had been returned to the New York office as unclaimed in Butte. The telegraph company reported that Mr. Jones was not to be found and that he had not been seen in Butte since the 3d of September. The lawyers were hourly expecting word from Montana men to whom they had telegraphed for information and advice. They were extremely nervous, but Montgomery Brewster was too eager and excited to notice the fact.

"A tall, bearded stranger was here this morning asking for you, Mr. Brewster," said Ripley, his head bent over some papers on his desk.

"Ah! Jones, I'm sure. I've always imagined him with a long beard," said Monty, relief in his voice.

"It was not Mr. Jones. We know Jones quite well. This man was a stranger and refused to give his name. He said he would call at Mrs. Gray's this afternoon."

"Did he look like a constable or a bill-collector?" asked Monty, with a laugh.

"He looked very much like a tramp."

"Well, we'll forget him for the time being," said Monty, drawing the report from his pocket. "Would you mind looking over this report, gentlemen? I'd like to know if it is in proper form to present to Mr. Jones."

Grant's hand trembled as he took the carefully folded sheet from Brewster. A quick glance of despair passed between the two lawyers.

"Of course, you'll understand that this report is merely a synopsis of the expenditures.

They are classified, however, and the receipts
over there are arranged in such a way that Mr.
Jones can very easily verify all the figures set
out in the report.   For instance, where it says
'cigars,' I have put down the total amount that
went up in smoke.   The receipts are to serve
as an itemized statement, you know."   Mr.
Ripley took the paper from his partner's hand
and, pulling himself together, read the report
aloud.   It was as follows:

New York, Sept. 23, 19—.
To SWEARENGEN JONES, ESQ.

Executor under the will of the late James
T. Sedgwick of Montana:

In pursuance of the terms of the aforesaid
will and in accord with the instructions set
forth by yourself as executor, I present my
report of receipts and disbursements for the
year in my life ending at midnight on Sept. 22.
The accuracy of the figures set forth in this
general statement may be established by referring to the receipts, which form a part of this
report.   There is not one penny of Edwin
Peter Brewster's money in my possession, and
I have no asset to mark its burial place.   These
figures are submitted for your most careful
consideration.

ORIGINAL CAPITAL . $1,000,000.00
"Lumber and Fuel" misfortune   58,550.00
Prize-fight misjudged . . .   1,000.00
Monte Carlo education . . .   40,000.00
Race track errors 700.00
Sale of six terrier pups   . .   150.00
Sale of furniture and personal
  effects 40,500.00
Interest on funds once in hand   19,140.00
                     —————

   Total amount to be disposed of   . . $1,160,040.00

DISBURSEMENTS

Rent for apartments   . . . $23,000.00
Furnishing apartments   . .   88,372.00
Three automobiles 21,000.00
Renting six automobiles   . .   25,000.00
Amount lost to DeMille   . .   1,000.00
Salaries 25,650.00
Amount paid to men injured
  in auto accident 12,240.00
Amount lost in bank failure .   113,468.25
Amount lost on races . . .   4,000.00
One glass screen 3,000.00
Christmas presents 7,211.00
Postage 1,105.00
Cable and telegraph   . . .   3,253.00
Stationery 2,400.00
Two Boston terriers   . . .   600.00
Amount lost to "hold-up men"   450.00
Amount lost on concert tour .   56,382.00
Amount lost through O. Har-
  rison's speculation (on my
  account) 60,000.00
One ball (in two sections)   .   60,000.00
Extra favors 6,000.00
One yacht cruise 212,309.50
One carnival 6,824.00
Cigars 1,720.00
Drinks, chiefly for others . .   9,040.00
Clothing 3,400.00

Rent of one villa	20,000.00
One courier	500.00
Dinner parties	117,900.00
Suppers and luncheons . .	38,000.00
Theater parties and suppers .	6,277.00
Hotel expenses	61,218.59
Railway and steamship fares	31,274.81
For Newsboys' Home . . .	5,000.00
Two opera performances . .	20,000.00
Repairs to "Flitter" . . .	6,342.60
In tow from somewhere to Southampton . . .	50,000.00
Special train to Florida . .	1,000.00
Cottage in Florida	5,500.00
Medical attendance	3,100.00
Living expenses in Florida .	8,900.00
Misappropriation of personal property by servants . .	3,580.00
Taxes on personal property .	112.25
Sundries	9,105.00
Household expenses . . .	24,805.00

Total disbursements $1,160,040.00
BALANCE ON HAND . . . $0,000,000.00
Respectfully submitted,
MONTGOMERY BREWSTER.

"It's rather broad, you see, gentlemen, but there are receipts for every dollar, barring some trifling incidentals. He may think I dissipated the fortune, but I defy him or anyone else to prove that I have not had my money's worth. To tell you the truth, it has seemed like a hundred million. If anyone should tell you that it is an easy matter to waste a million dollars, refer him to me. Last fall I weighed 180 pounds, yesterday I barely moved the beam at 140; last fall there was not a wrinkle in my face, nor did I have a white hair. You see the result of overwork, gentlemen. It will take an age to get back to where I was physically, but I think I can do it with the vacation that begins to-morrow. Incidentally, I'm going to be married to-morrow morning, just when I am poorer than I ever expect to be again. I still have a few dollars to spend and I must be about it. To-morrow I will account for what I spend this evening. It is now covered by the 'sundries' item, but I'll have the receipts to show, all right. See you to-morrow morning.''

He was gone, eager to be with Peggy, afraid to discuss his report with the lawyers. Grant and Ripley shook their heads and sat silent for a long time after his departure.

"We ought to hear something definite before night," said Grant, but there was anxiety in his voice.

"I wonder," mused Ripley, as if to himself, "how he will take it if the worst should happen."

CHAPTER XXXII

THE NIGHT BEFORE

"It's all up to Jones now," kept running through Brewster's brain as he drove off to keep his appointment with Peggy Gray. "The million is gone—all gone. I'm as poor as Job's turkey. It's up to Jones, but I don't see how he can decide against me. He insisted on making a pauper of me and he can t have the heart to throw me down now. But, what if he should take it into his head to be ugly! I wonder if I could break the will—I wonder if I could beat him out in court."

Peggy was waiting for him. Her cheeks were flushed as with a fever. She had caught from him the mad excitement of the occasion.

"Come, Peggy," he exclaimed, eagerly. "This is our last holiday—let's be merry. We can forget it to-morrow, if you like, when we begin all over again, but maybe it will be worth remembering." He assisted her to the seat and then leaped up beside her. "We're off!" he cried, his voice quivering.

"It is absolute madness, dear," she said,

but her eyes were sparkling with the joy of recklessness. Away went the trap and the two light hearts. Mrs. Gray turned from a window in the house with tears in her eyes. To her troubled mind they were driving off into utter darkness.

"The queerest looking man came to the house to see you this afternoon, Monty," said Peggy. "He wore a beard and he made me think of one of Remington's cowboys."

"What was his name?"

"He told the maid it did not matter. I saw him as he walked away and he looked very much a man. He said he would come to-morrow if he did not find you down town to-night. Don't you recognize him from the description?"

"Not at all. Can't imagine who he is."

"Monty," she said, after a moment's painful reflection, "he—he couldn't have been a——"

"I know what you mean. An officer sent up to attach my belongings or something of the sort. No, dearest; I give you my word of honor I do not owe a dollar in the world." Then he recalled his peculiar indebtedness to Bragdon and Gardner. "Except one or two very small personal obligations," he added, hastily. "Don't worry about it, dear, we are out for a good time and we must make the most of it. First, we drive through the Park, then we dine at Sherry's."

"But we must dress for that, dear," she cried. "And the chaperon?"

He turned very red when she spoke of dressing. "I'm ashamed to confess it, Peggy, but I have no other clothes than these I'm wearing now. Don't look so hurt, dear—I'm going to leave an order for new evening clothes to-morrow—if I have the time. And about the chaperon. People won't be talking before to-morrow and by that time——"

"No, Monty, Sherry's is out of the question. We can't go there," she said, decisively.

"Oh, Peggy! That spoils everything," he cried, in deep disappointment.

"It isn't fair to me, Monty. Everybody would know us and every tongue would wag. They would say, 'There are Monty Brewster and Margaret Gray. Spending his last few dollars on her.' You wouldn't have them think that?"

He saw the justice in her protest. "A quiet little dinner in some out of the way place would be joyous," she added, persuasively.

"You're right, Peggy, you're always right. You see, I'm so used to spending money by the handful that I don't know how to do it any other way. I believe I'll let you carry the pocketbook after to-morrow. Let me think; I know a nice little restaurant down town. We'll go there and then to the theater. Dan DeMille and his wife are to be in my box and we're all going up to Pettingill's studio afterward. I'm to give the 'Little Sons' a farewell supper. If my calculations don't go wrong, that will be the end of the jaunt and we'll go home happy."

At eleven o'clock Pettingill's studio opened its doors to the "Little Sons" and their guests, and the last "Dutch lunch" was soon under way. Brewster had paid for it early in the evening and when he sat down at the head of the table there was not a penny in his pockets. A year ago, at the same place and at the same hour, he and the "Little Sons" were having a birthday feast. A million dollars came to him on that night. To-night he was poorer by far than on the other occasion, but he expected a little gift on the new anniversary.

Around the board, besides the nine "Little Sons," sat six guests, among them the DeMilles, Peggy Gray and Mary Valentine. "Nopper" Harrison was the only absent "Little Son" and his health was proposed by Brewster almost before the echoes of the toast to the bride and groom died away.

Interruption came earlier on this occasion than it did that night a year ago. Ellis did not deliver his messages to Brewster until three o'clock in the morning, but the A.D.T. boy who rang the bell at Pettingill's a year later handed him a telegram before twelve o'clock.

"Congratulations are coming in, old man," said DeMille, as Monty looked fearfully at the little envelope the boy had given him.

"Many happy returns of the day," suggested Bragdon. "By Jove, it's sensible of you to get married on your birthday, Monty. It saves time and expense to your friends."

"Read it aloud," said "Subway" Smith.

"Two to one it's from Nopper Harrison," cried Pettingill.

Brewster's fingers trembled, he knew not why, as he opened the envelope. There was the most desolate feeling in his heart, the most ghastly premonition that ill-news had come in this last hour. He drew forth the telegram and slowly painfully unfolded it. No one could have told by his expression that he felt almost that he was reading his death warrant. It was from Grant & Ripley and evidently had been following him about town for two or three hours. The lawyers had filed it at 8:30 o'clock.

He read it at a glance, his eyes burning, his heart freezing. To the end of his days these words lived sharp and distinct in his brain.

"Come to the office immediately. Will wait all night for you if necessary. Jones has disappeared and there is absolutely no trace of him.   Grant & Ripley."

Brewster sat as one paralyzed, absolutely no sign of emotion in his face. The others began to clamor for the contents of the telegram, but his tongue was stiff and motionless, his ears deaf. Every drop of blood in his body was stilled by the shock, every sense given him by the Creator was centered upon eleven words in the handwriting of a careless telegraph operator—"Jones has disappeared and there is absolutely no trace of him."

"JONES HAS DISAPPEARED!" Those were the words, plain and terrible in their clearness, tremendous in their brutality. Slowly the rest of the message began to urge its claims upon his brain. "Come to our office immediately" and "Will wait all night" battled for recognition. He was calm because he had not the power to express an emotion. How he

maintained control of himself afterward he
never knew. Some powerful, kindly force
asserted itself, coming to his relief with the
timeliness of a genii. Gradually it began to
dawn upon him that the others were waiting
for him to read the message aloud. He was
not sure that a sound would come forth when
he opened his lips to speak, but the tones were
steady, natural and as cold as steel.

"I am sorry I can't tell you about this," he
said, so gravely that his hearers were silenced.
"It is a business matter of such vital importance that I must ask you to excuse me for an
hour or so. I will explain everything to-morrow. Please don't be uneasy. If you will do
me the honor to grace the board of an absent
host, I'll be most grateful. It is imperative
that I go, and at once. I promise to return in
an hour." He was standing, his knees as stiff
as iron.

"Is it anything serious?" asked DeMille.

"What! has anything happened?" came in
halting, frightened tones from Peggy.

"It concerns me alone, and it is purely of a
business nature. Seriously, I can't delay going
for another minute. It is vital. In an hour
I'll return. Peggy, don't be worried—don't
be distressed about me. Go on and have a

good time, everybody, and you'll find me the
jolliest fellow of all when I come back. It's
twelve o'clock. I'll be here by one on the 23d
of September.''

"Let me go with you," pleaded Peggy, trem-
ulously, as she followed him into the hallway.

"I must go alone," he answered. "Don't
worry, little woman, it will be all right.''

His kiss sent a chill to the very bottom of
Peggy's heart.

CHAPTER XXXIII

THE FLIGHT OF JONES

Everything seemed like a dream to Brewster as he rushed off through the night to the office of Grant & Ripley. He was dazed, bewildered, hardly more than half-conscious. A bitter smile crept about his lips as he drew away from the street-car track almost as his hand touched the rail of a car he had signaled. He remembered that he did not have money enough to pay his fare. It was six or seven blocks to the office of the lawyers, and he was actually running before he stopped at the entrance of the big building.

Never had an elevator traveled more slowly than the one which shot him to the seventh floor. A light shone through the transom above the attorneys' door and he entered without so much as a rap on the panel. Grant, who was pacing the floor, came to a standstill and faced his visitor.

"Close the door, please," came in steady tones from Ripley. Mr. Grant dropped into a chair and Brewster mechanically slammed the door.

"Is it true?" he demanded hoarsely, his hand still on the knob.

"Sit down, Brewster, and control yourself," said Ripley.

"Good God, man, can't you see I am calm?" cried Monty. "Go on—tell me all about it. What do you know? What have you heard?"

"He cannot be found, that's all," announced Ripley, with deadly intentness. "I don't know what it means. There is no explanation. The whole thing is inconceivable. Sit down and I will tell you everything as quickly as possible."

"There isn't much to tell," said Grant, mechanically.

"I can take it better standing," declared Brewster, shutting his jaws tightly.

"Jones was last seen in Butte on the third of this month," said Ripley. "We sent several telegrams to him after that day, asking when he expected to leave for New York. They never were claimed and the telegraph company reported that he could not be found. We thought he might have gone off to look after some of his property and were not uneasy. Finally we began to wonder why he had not wired us on leaving for the east. I telegraphed again and got no answer. It dawned

upon us that this was something unusual.   We
wired his secretary and received a response
from the chief of police.   He asked, in turn,
if we could tell him anything about the whereabouts of Jones.   This naturally alarmed us
and yesterday we kept the wires hot.   The
result of our inquiries is terrible, Mr. Brewster."

"Why didn't you tell me?" asked Brewster.

"There can be no doubt that Jones has fled,
accompanied by his secretary.   The belief in
Butte is that the secretary has murdered him."

"God!" was the only sound that came from
the lips of Brewster.

Ripley moistened his lips and went on.

"We have dispatches here from the police,
the banks, the trust companies and from a half
dozen mine managers.   You may read them
if you like, but I can tell you what they say.
About the first of this month Jones began to
turn various securities into money.   It is now
known that they were once the property of
James T. Sedgwick, held in trust for you.   The
safety deposit vaults were afterward visited and
inspection shows that he removed every scrap
of stock, every bond, everything of value
that he could lay his hands upon.   His own
papers and effects were not disturbed.   Yours
alone have disappeared.   It is this fact that

convinces the authorities that the secretary has made away with the old man and has fled with the property. The bank people say that Jones drew out every dollar of the Sedgwick money, and the police say that he realized tremendous sums on the convertible securities. The strange part of it is that he sold your mines and your real estate, the purchaser being a man named Golden. Brewster, it—it looks very much as if he had disappeared with everything.''

Brewster did not take his eyes from Ripley's face throughout the terrible speech; he did not move a fraction of an inch from the rigid position assumed at the beginning.

"Is anything being done?" he asked, mechanically.

"The police are investigating. He is known to have started off into the mountains with this secretary, on the third of September. Neither has been seen since that day, so far as anyone knows. The earth seems to have swallowed them. The authorities are searching the mountains and are making every effort to find Jones or his body. He is known to be eccentric and at first not much importance was attached to his actions. That is all we can tell you at present. There may be developments to-morrow. It looks bad—terribly bad. We— we had the utmost confidence in Jones. My God, I wish I could help you, my boy.''

"I don't blame you, gentlemen,'' said Brewster, bravely. "It's just my luck, that's all. Something told me all along that—that it wouldn't turn out right. I wasn't looking for this kind of end, though. My only fear was that—Jones wouldn't consider me worthy to receive the fortune. It never occurred to me that he might prove to be the—the unworthy one.''

"I will take you a little farther into our confidence, Brewster,'' said Grant, slowly. "Mr. Jones notified us in the beginning that he would be governed largely in his decision by our opinion of your conduct. That is why we felt no hesitation in advising you to continue as you were going. While you were off at sea, we had many letters from him, all in that sarcastic vein of his, but in none of them did he offer a word of criticism. He seemed thoroughly satisfied with your methods. In fact, he once said he'd give a million of his own money if it would purchase your ability to spend one-fourth of it.''

"Well, he can have my experience free of charge. A beggar can't be a chooser, you know," said Brewster, bitterly. His color was gradually coming back. "What do they know about the secretary?" he asked, suddenly, intent and alive.

"He was a new one, I understand, who came to Jones less than a year ago. Jones is said to have had implicit faith in him," said Ripley.

"And he disappeared at the same time?"

"They were last seen together."

"Then, he has put an end to Jones!" cried Monty, excitedly. "It is as plain as day to me. Don't you see that he exerted some sort of influence over the old man, inducing him to get all this money together on some pretext or other, solely for the purpose of robbing him of the whole amount? Was ever anything more diabolical?" He began pacing the floor like an animal, nervously clasping and unclasping his hands. "We must catch that secretary! I don't believe Jones was dishonest. He has been duped by a clever scoundrel."

"The strangest circumstance of all, Mr. Brewster, is that no such person as Golden, the purchaser of your properties, can be found. He is supposed to reside in Omaha, and it is known that he paid nearly three million dollars for the property that now stands in his name. He paid it to Mr. Jones in cash, too, and he paid every cent that the property is worth."

"But he must be in existence somewhere," cried Brewster, in perplexity. "How the devil could he pay the money if he doesn't exist?"

"I only know that no trace of the man can be found. They know nothing of him in Omaha," said Grant, helplessly.

"So it has finally happened," said Brewster, but his excitement had dropped. "Well," he added, throwing himself into a deep chair, "it was always much too strange to be true. Even at the beginning it seemed like a dream, and now—well, now I am just awake, like the little boy after the fairy-tale. I seem like a fool to have taken it so seriously."

"There was no other way," protested Ripley, "you were quite right."

"Well, after all," continued Brewster, and the voice was as of one in a dream, "perhaps it's as well to have been in Wonderland even if you have to come down afterward to the ordinary world. I am foolish, perhaps, but even now I would not give it up." Then the thought of Peggy clutched him by the throat, and he stopped. After a moment he gathered himself together and rose. "Gentlemen," he said sharply, and his voice had changed; "I

have had my fun and this is the end of it.
Down underneath I am desperately tired of
the whole thing, and I give you my word that
you will find me a different man to-morrow.
I am going to buckle down to the real thing.
I am going to prove that my grandfather's
blood is in me. And I shall come out on top."

Ripley was obviously moved as he replied,
"I don't question it for a moment. You are
made of the right stuff. I saw that long ago.
You may count on us to-morrow for any amount
you need."

Grant endorsed the opinion. "I like your
spirit, Brewster," he said. "There are not
many men who would have taken this as well.
It's pretty hard on you, too, and it's a miserable
wedding gift for your bride."

"We may have important news from Butte
in the morning," said Ripley, hopefully; "at
any rate, more of the details. The newspapers
will have sensational stories no doubt, and we
have asked for the latest particulars direct from
the authorities. We'll see that things are
properly investigated. Go home now, my boy,
and go to bed. You will begin to-morrow with
good luck at your side and you may be happy
all your life in spite of to-night's depression."

"I'm sure to be happy," said Brewster,

simply. "The ceremony takes place at seven o'clock, gentlemen. I was coming to your office at nine on a little matter of business, but I fancy it won't after all be necessary for me to hurry. I'll drop in before noon, however, and get that money. By the way, here are the receipts for the money I spent to-night. Will you put them away with the others? I intend to live up to my part of the contract, and it will save me the trouble of presenting them regularly in the morning. Good night, gentlemen. I am sorry you were obliged to stay up so late on my account."

He left them bravely enough, but he had more than one moment of weakness before he could meet his friends. The world seemed unreal and himself the most unreal thing in it. But the night air acted as a stimulant and helped him to call back his courage. When he entered the studio at one o'clock, he was prepared to redeem his promise to be "the jolliest fellow of them all."

CHAPTER XXXIV

THE LAST WORD

"I'll tell you about it later, dear," was all that Peggy, pleading, could draw from him.

At midnight Mrs. Dan had remonstrated with her. "You must go home, Peggy dear," she said. "It is disgraceful for you to stay up so late. I went to bed at eight o'clock the night before I was married."

"And fell asleep at four in the morning," smiled Peggy.

"You are quite mistaken, my dear. I did not fall asleep at all. But I won't allow you to stop a minute longer. It puts rings under the eyes and sometimes they're red the morning after."

"Oh, you dear sweet philosopher," cried Peggy; "how wise you are. Do you think I need a beauty sleep?"

"I don't want you to be a sleepy beauty, that's all," retorted Mrs. Dan.

Upon Monty's return from his trying hour with the lawyers, he had been besieged with questions, but he was cleverly evasive. Peggy alone was insistent; she had curbed her curiosity until they were on the way home, and then she implored him to tell her what had happened. The misery he had endured was as nothing to this reckoning with the woman who had the right to expect fair treatment. His duty was clear, but the strain had been heavy and it was not easy to meet it.

"Peggy, something terrible has happened," he faltered, uncertain of his course.

"Tell me everything, Monty, you can trust me to be brave."

"When I asked you to marry me," he continued gravely, "it was with the thought that I could give you everything to-morrow. I looked for a fortune. I never meant that you should marry a pauper."

"I don't understand. You tried to test my love for you?"

"No, child, not that. But I was pledged not to speak of the money I expected, and I wanted you so much before it came."

"And it has failed you?" she answered. "I can't see that it changes things. I expected to marry a pauper, as you call it. Do you think this could make a difference?"

"But you don't understand, Peggy. I haven't a penny in the world."

"You hadn't a penny when I accepted you," she replied. "I am not afraid. I believe in you. And if you love me I shall not give you up."

"Dearest!"and the carriage was at the door before another word was uttered. But Monty called to the coachman to drive just once around the block.

"Good night, my darling," he said when they reached home. "Sleep till eight o'clock if you like. There is nothing now in the way of having the wedding at nine, instead of at seven. In fact, I have a reason for wanting my whole fortune to come to me then. You will be all that I have in the world, child, but I am the happiest man alive."

In his room the strain was relaxed and Brewster faced the bitter reality. Without undressing he threw himself upon the lounge and wondered what the world held for him. It held Peggy at least, he thought, and she was enough. But had he been fair to her? Was he right in exacting a sacrifice? His tired brain whirled in the effort to decide. Only one thing was clear—that he could not give her up. The future grew black at the very thought of it. With her he could make things go, but alone it was another matter. He

would take the plunge and he would justify it.
His mind went traveling back over the graceless year, and he suddenly realized that he had
forfeited the confidence of men who were
worth while.   His course in profligacy would
not be considered the best training for business.
The thought nerved him to action.   He must
make good.   Peggy had faith in him.   She
came to him when everything was against him,
and he would slave for her, he would starve, he
would do anything to prove that she was not
mistaken in him.   She at least should know
him for a man.

Looking toward the window he saw the
black, uneasy night give way to the coming
day.   Haggard and faint he arose from the
couch to watch the approach of the sun that is
indifferent to wealth and poverty, to gayety
and dejection.   From far off in the gray light
there came the sound of a five o'clock bell.   A
little later the shrieks of factory whistles were
borne to his ears, muffled by distance but
pregnant with the importance of a new day of
toil.   They were calling him, with all poor
men, to the sweat-shop and the forge, to the
great mill of life.   The new era had begun,
dawning bright and clear to disperse the gloom
in his soul.   Leaning against the casement and

wondering where he could earn the first dollar for the Peggy Brewster that was Peggy Gray, he rose to meet it with a fine unflinching fearlessness.

Before seven o'clock he was down stairs and waiting. Joe Bragdon joined him a bit later, followed by Gardner and the minister. The DeMilles appeared without an invitation, but they were not denied. Mrs. Dan sagely shook her head when told that Peggy was still asleep and that the ceremony was off till nine o'clock.

"Monty, are you going away?" asked Dan, drawing him into a corner.

"Just a week in the hills," answered Monty, suddenly remembering the generosity of his attorneys.

"Come in and see me as soon as you return, old man," said DeMille, and Monty knew that a position would be open to him.

To Mrs. Dan fell the honor of helping Peggy dress. By the time she had had coffee and was ready to go down, she was pink with excitement and had quite forgotten the anxiety which had made the night an age.

She had never been prettier than on her wedding morning. Her color was rich, her eyes as clear as stars, her woman's body the picture of grace and health. Monty's heart leaped high with love of her.

"The prettiest girl in New York, by Jove," gasped Dan DeMille, clutching Bragdon by the arm.

"And look at Monty! He's become a new man in the last five minutes," added Joe. Look at the glow in his cheeks! By the eternal, he's beginning to look as he did a year ago."

A clock chimed the hour of nine.

*   *   *   *   *   *   *   *   *

"The man who was here yesterday is in the hall to see Mr. Brewster," said the maid, a few minutes after the minister had uttered the words that gave Peggy a new name. There was a moment of silence, almost of dread.

"You mean the fellow with the beard?" asked Monty, uneasily.

"Yes, sir. He sent in this letter, begging you to read it at once.

"Shall I send him away, Monty?" demanded Bragdon, defiantly. "What does he mean by coming at this time?"

"I'll read the letter first, Joe."

Every eye was on Brewster as he tore open the envelope. His face was expressive. There was wonder in it, then incredulity, then joy. He threw the letter to Bragdon, clasped Peggy in his arms spasmodically, and then, releasing her, dashed for the hall like one bereft of reason.

"It's Nopper Harrison!" he cried, and a moment later the tall visitor was dragged into the circle. "Nopper" was quite overcome by the heartiness of his welcome.

"You are an angel, Nopper, God bless you!" said Monty, with convincing emphasis. "Joe, read that letter aloud and then advertize for the return of those Boston terriers!"

Bragdon's hands trembled and his voice was not sure as he translated the scrawl, "Nopper" Harrison standing behind him for the gleeful purpose of prompting him when the writing was beyond the range of human intelligence.

"Holland House, Sept. 23, 19—
"Mr. Montgomery Brewster,
"My Dear Boy:
"So you thought I had given you the slip, eh? Didn't think I'd show up here and do my part? Well, I don't blame you; I suppose I've acted like a damned idiot, but so long as it turns out O.K. there's no harm done. The wolf won't gnaw very much of a hole in your door, I reckon. This letter introduces my

secretary, Mr. Oliver Harrison. He came to me last June, out in Butte, with the prospectus of a claim he had staked out up in the mountains. What he wanted was backing and he had such a good show to win out that I went into cahoots with him. He's got a mine up there that is dead sure to yield millions. Seems as though he has to give you half of the yield, though. Says you grub-staked him. Good fellow, this Harrison. Needed a secretary and man of affairs, so took him into my office. You can see that he did not take me up into the mountains to murder me, as the papers say this morning. Damned rot. Nobody's business but my own if I concluded to come east without telling everybody in Butte about it.

"I am here and so is the money. Got in last night. Harrison came from Chicago a day ahead of me. I went to office of G. & R. at eight this morning. Found them in a hell of a stew. Thought I'd skipped out or been murdered. Money all gone, everything gone to smash. That's what they thought. Don't blame 'em much. You see it was this way: I concluded to follow out the terms of the will and deliver the goods in person. I got together all of Jim Sedgwick's stuff and did a lot of other fool things, I suppose, and hiked

off to New York. You'll find about seven
million dollars' worth of stuff to your credit
when you endorse the certified checks down at
Grant & Ripley's, my boy. It's all here and
in the banks.

"It's a mighty decent sort of wedding gift, I
reckon.

"The lawyers told me all about you. Told
me all about last night, and that you were
going to be married this morning. By this
time you're comparatively happy with the
bride, I guess. I looked over your report and
took a few peeps at the receipts. They're all
right. I'm satisfied. The money is yours.
Then I got to thinking that maybe you wouldn't
care to come down at nine o'clock, especially
as you are just recovering from the joy of being
married, so I settled with the lawyers and
they'll settle with you. If you have nothing in
particular to do this afternoon about two
o'clock, I'd suggest that you come to the hotel
and we'll dispose of a few formalities that the
law requires of us. And you can give me some
lessons in spending money. I've got a little
I'd like to miss some morning. As for your
ability as a business man, I have this to say:
Any man who can spend a million a year and
have nothing to show for it, don't need a

recommendation from anybody. He's in a class by himself and it's a business that no one else can give him a pointer about. The best test of your real capacity, my boy, is the way you listed your property for taxation. It's a true sign of business sagacity. That would have decided me in your favor if everything else had been against you.

"I'm sorry you've been worried about all this. You have gone through a good deal in a year and you have been roasted from Hades to breakfast by everybody. Now it's your turn to laugh. It will surprise them to read the "extras" to-day. I've done my duty to you in more ways than one. I've got myself interviewed by the newspapers and to-day they'll print the whole truth about Montgomery Brewster and his millions. They've got the Sedgwick will and my story and the old town will boil with excitement. I guess you'll be squared before the world, all right. You'd better stay indoors for awhile though, if you want to have a quiet honeymoon.

"I don't like New York. Never did. Am going back to Butte to-night. Out there we have real sky-scrapers and they are not built of brick. They are two or three miles high and they have gold in 'em. There is real grass in the lowlands and we have valleys that make Central Park look like a half an inch of nothing. Probably you and Mrs. Brewster were going to take a wedding trip, so why not go west with me in my car? We start at 7:45 P.M. and I won't bother you. Then you can take it anywhere you like.

"Sincerely yours,
"Swearengen Jones.

"P.S. I forgot to say there is no such man as Golden. I bought your mines and ranches with my own money. You may buy them back at the same figures. I'd advise you to do it. They'll be worth twice as much in a year. I hope you'll forgive the whims of an old man who has liked you from the start.   J."

THE END.